Blair: Encouraged to Believe

The Barnabas Chronicles
Book 3

By

Ronna M. Bacon

Jeremiah 29:13
And you will seek Me and find Me, when you search for Me with all your heart.
NKJV

Table of Contents

Chapter 1

Shrugging deeper into his red and black plaid winter jacket and tugging his woollen hat further down over his ears and his light brown curls, Blair Campion studied the vehicle perched precariously on the side of the road, nose down into the ditch. He shook his head as he slipped from behind the wheel of his truck, his feet sliding slightly on the icy mess underfoot. He caught himself, drawing in his breath, knowing if he fell, he would have trouble getting back up. The sleet and snow had accumulated during the day, and he didn't envy the tow truck driver the task of pulling out the car ahead of him. He himself had been late getting away from the garage where he worked as a mechanic.

Blair ducked his head to glance into the window on the driver's side, opening the door and closing it again, before he studied the ground once more. Whoever had been driving seemed to have made it out, he thought. Now to find them. They wouldn't survive for long, he thought, not in this weather if they were out in the open. His warm brown eyes searched the area, finding indentations he thought were footsteps. His eyes moved constantly as he walked slowly forward, stepping to the side as he saw the lights of an approaching vehicle. Recognizing it, he raised a hand and then moved to stand at the driver's door of the truck as it stopped beside him.

"Bradon? Branigan? What are you two doing out here?" He watched closely as his friends and teammates exchanged glances.

The three were part of a group of men whose salaries were paid for by The Barnabas Foundation, a foundation operated by Barnabas Carey. By paying their salaries, Barnabas made it possible for their employers to hire others to work in their businesses without having to worry about finding the money for their wages. The men also volunteered in various capacities.

"Looking for you?" Bradon grinned, an arm resting on the driver's door, his other hand on the steering wheel. "Anna, Doc's wife, was worried about you. She said you had promised to be home in time to eat with them and you're late."

"That's right, I was." Blair groaned. "I had to finish off a vehicle before I left, and then I found that." His thumb pointed behind him.

"Found what?" Branigan stared past him, his eyes narrowing. "That car? There shouldn't be any vehicles on this road."

"I know. The driver's not there. And it looks like they were run off the road. We'll need to call it in." Blair turned back to face the car. "I had just started searching when you came along." He stared down at the work boots he was wearing. "Except I'm not exactly dressed for the weather."

Bradon stared at the car and then moved to open his door. "I didn't bring Kade. I should have." He was referring to his dog, who was trained in search and rescue. "We'll search, and if I have to, I'll go get him."

"Thanks, guys."

The three spread out, finally meeting by the car once more.

"We'll have to call it in." Blair swiped at the sleet on his face. "Whoever it is can't survive much longer."

"I called it in already, Blair." Bradon stopped for a moment, stooping to peer at the car. "This isn't good." He spun. "Which way would they have gone?"

"We're assuming that they are still here, aren't we? What happens if they were pulled into the other vehicle and disappeared?" Branigan was running scenarios through his mind.

"That's what I'm afraid has happened." Blair spun in a circle, seeing the red and blue flashing lights of the emergency vehicles as they approached. "There's John with the tow truck as well. He'll take it back to work for us."

"Once it's released. That doesn't solve this." Bradon moved away, his eyes down. "I almost need to go and bring Kade back."

They all turned to the responding officers, answering as best they could, before looking up to see another friend, Brady Coghlan, standing near the paramedic rig.

"Brady's here." Branigan Clery's voice was low.

"So he is. He'll have had a busy day, no doubt." Bradon Cahill responded. "Now, let's spread out more. We've checked the ditches. Let's check on the other side."

The three men conferred with the officers, who nodded, knowing the men Barnabas employed. Blair searched once more around the car and then stood, his eyes on the trees, a thoughtful look on his face.

"Blair?"

He turned as Brady spoke from beside him. "Brady? Glad you're here."

"No sign of the driver?" Brady winced as he looked at the car. "That's not good."

"No, no sign." Blair sighed to himself, offering a prayer for their own safety and the safety of whoever it had been in the car. "We're not even sure the driver is still around."

Brady nodded. "I see. How about we look up in the trees? Maybe they made it that far and have hidden themselves."

Blair nodded, heading that way, slipping and sliding down the slope to the ditch and then back up the other side. Brady watched him closely, eyeing his footwear and then shaking his head. He knew Blair had just reacted to the situation, not thinking about his own safety. But then again, Lord, he muttered, we all do. We've already proven that with Baird and Berneen and Benen and Cadee, haven't we? You protected them. Now, please, protect us?

Blair ducked under the low-lying branches, thick with sleet and wet snow, and stared around, standing still for a moment before Brady's hand touched his arm.

"This way, Blair. I can see tracks that haven't been covered."

Blair frowned. "It has to be a woman. Those tracks are too small to be a man's."

"That they are." Brady was suddenly running forward, dropping to his knees beside a still form. "Blair, go get Tom. I've found our driver. Then, I need you to stay back." Brady looked around, catching the nod of acknowledgement before Blair turned and moved as quickly as he could away from the area.

Blair stood, anxious for some reason, his heart raised in prayer, his eyes on the area that he had just returned from, Branigan and Bradon on either side of him. They watched as the police officers milled around, finally releasing the vehicle for the tow truck to remove.

Blair moved forward as he saw the stretcher gently lowered to the road and then raised to full height as Brady and his partner moved forward to the paramedic rig, his eyes on the form laying so still. He frowned. Something was familiar about the person.

Brady watched closely as Blair approached, his mouth open to speak before he snapped it closely, his puzzled eyes turning to Branigan and Bradon, who both shrugged.

Blair stood for a moment, his eyes on the lady laying there, his heart sinking. He knew her. His hand reached out to touch the dark auburn hair, willing her curiously-coloured jade eyes to open.

—

"I need to go with her, Brady." He finally spoke.

"You can't, Blair." Brady was puzzled as to Blair's reaction.

"I have to, Brady. She's a friend." Blair didn't feel the hands on his arms as Branigan and Bradon both reached to restrain his movements and move him backwards.

"It still doesn't matter, Blair. You can't go with her."

"She's a really good friend, Brady. I have to."

Brady and his partner shared a look, Tom shaking his head and motioning towards the rig.

"Blair, come on. You can't go with her. We need you to step back." Brady waited but Blair made no effort to move. "Blair? Come on. Please? Let us load the lady and go."

"I have to go with her, Brady." Blair looked up, his friends drawing in their breath at the look of devastation, worry, concern and something unreadable in his eyes.

"You can't, Blair. Now, move." Brady nodded to the other two men, who once more gently restrained Blair from moving forward.

"I have to, Brady. I just have to." Blair's eyes were on the lady's hand, studying the rose quartz ring on her finger, before Brady tucked her hand back under the blanket. "I have to go with her."

"No, you don't. Why are you so adamant about this? You've never mentioned her. We've never seen her before." Brady nodded to Tom and then began to load the stretcher, pausing as Blair was up and into the rig and seated in a corner. "Blair?"

"I have to, Brady." He looked up, once more the unreadable expression in his eyes and on his face. "You see, I know her well. She's my fiancee."

His words stunned the four men, causing them to stare at each other, before they stared at Blair, who didn't see the looks, his eyes back on Devaney Daubney, who had disappeared from his life just as their college days ended, and before they had finalized the plans for their wedding. When had she come to Ontario from Alberta, he wondered? And why be on this road?

Chapter 2

Barnabas Carey stood in the hospital corridor a number of hours later, his eyes on Blair as he paced, occasionally stopping to stare at the closed room door. He shook his head. Hadn't he just done this, Lord? Stood and watched one of his friends do almost the same thing? Was Blair to go through what Benen and Baird had? Please, Lord, protect him. Protect this lady he claims to know.

Branigan and Bradon flanked him, not sure what to say. They had relayed Blair's reaction and actions to Barnabas who had stared at them and then turned to study Blair.

"He said what?" Barnabas was not sure he had heard correctly.

"He told us she was his fiancee. I have never heard him mention her at all." Branigan shrugged, his thoughts muddled. "What has he gone and got involved in?"

"Another Baird. Another Benen." Bradon's droll comment brought brief smiles to the men's faces before Barnabas walked forward, the other two men keeping step with him.

"Blair?" Barnabas waited for Blair to respond. When he didn't, he deliberately stepped into his way, causing Blair to stop abruptly and stare at Barnabas.

"Barnabas? What are you doing here?" Blair was puzzled, his gaze going to the other two men, and then past them to Brady who was walking their way, his shift finished.

"I came to see a friend who needs me. Blair? Talk to me. Who is she?" Barnabas' hand on his arm drew Blair to a chair where he could still see the door.

"Devaney. We dated through college. We were to marry when we finished, but she just disappeared with no word, other than a note that said she had to do something and would be in touch. That's the last I heard. I've tried to find her." Blair rubbed at his hair and then his face, a hand resting for a moment on his cheek. "I don't think you knew. I was ready to tell you when you offered me the work here, but by that time, she was gone." His emotions were all over the place, he thought. Lord, I need to talk to her, but I am not sure what to say, or even if she'll want to see me.

"I knew something was up with you, but didn't know you well enough to ask." Barnabas studied his friend, close in age to himself. "It's been what? Six years or so?"

Blair nodded. "Almost that. She would have turned 29 last month." He shifted on the seat, uncomfortable at sitting when he wanted to be at her side. "Doc's the one who is treating her. He said he'd come get me."

"Was she hurt in the accident?" Branigan spoke up, his eyes first on Blair and then Brady, who was shaking his head.

"No, he said not. But she's not herself. I can see that. She's changed. And I want to know why and who did it."

His friends could hear the anger and worry in his voice. None of them knew quite how to respond to him. The four of his friends exchanged glances, not having seen Blair like this. They were not sure how to address him.

Brady had opened his mouth to speak when Doc approached, motioning for Blair to stay sitting. Doc sank down wearily. He had already worked a full shift and had been about to head for home when he was asked to stay. Some of the scheduled staff had not been able to get in with the weather, which was worsening. He didn't worry about Anna, knowing she was safe, but he worried about his young friends here, knowing they would want to leave as soon as they could.

He shook his head at Barnabas' questioning look before he searched Blair's face, frowning at what he saw there.

"Blair? Talk to me. How do you know this young lady?" Doc's voice was low and compassionate. All of the younger men living in the Foundation building were like sons to Anna and himself, and he cared deeply what was going on in their lives. He prayed for them daily, but right now, Blair was the focus of that prayer. He had called Anna earlier, just asking her to pray for Blair, without any details. Anna didn't need that, she had always maintained.

"Doc? How is she?" Blair refused to answer the question Doc had asked, worried about his lady.

"She's under treatment and has some imaging to undergo. She's not awake yet, if that's what you're asking." He sighed, knowing Blair was avoiding the question he had asked. "Blair? I need to know some things about your relationship with her before I can let you go see her. I know you told your friends she was your fiancee. You have never mentioned that to any of us, not in all the years we have known you."

Blair stared down at the floor, his eyes tracking the lines of the tiles, not sure how to respond, how much Devaney would want him to say. He finally looked up at Doc, not seeing the compassionate, caring looks on the faces of his friends.

"We've known each other for years. We ended up in the same foster home. She has always been in foster care. She never knew who her parents were. She was abandoned as a baby, with a birth certificate. When we tried to trace her parents, we didn't get very far. She's had a tough life, her foster experience not being great until she ended up in the one I was in. I ended up in that one when my mother disappeared. We tried to trace her as well, with no success. From what I can find out, my father died in an accident before I was born.

"Devaney and I went to the same college. We were friends, fell in love, and decided to marry once we were through college. We had most of our plans made, just needed to get the license, and we were going to do that right after graduation. I went to find her the next day after graduation and she was gone." Blair sighed, his head going back and his eyes closing, memories still sharp, brittle and hurting even after all those years.

"You tried to find her?" Doc's voice was certain on that.

"I did, Doc. I tried so hard. She hid herself well. I don't know where she went. I traced her to the bus station but I couldn't find out what bus she had taken or where she was heading. They wouldn't or couldn't tell me." He looked around at his friends, not sure what to expect. "I'm sorry, guys. I should have told you, but just couldn't."

"Not a problem, Blair." Brady spoke for the four. "We understand. You moved across the country right after that, not knowing where she was. That must have been hard."

Blair nodded. "It was. I felt like I had abandoned her. Our foster mother has kept in touch. She said she thought she saw her about six months ago, but couldn't be certain of that."

Doc looked up as a nurse approached and then rose, walking away for a moment, before he turned and watched Blair. He finally nodded, walking slowly back towards the younger man.

"Blair? You can come with me for a moment. I'll let you in to see her, but if she says you have to leave, you'll have to."

Chapter 3

Devaney Daubney roused, feeling warm for the first time in months, she thought, but disoriented. She cracked open her eyes, scanning quickly as she had become accustomed to doing, not seeing the man who had been haunting her for the last few years. She opened her eyes wider, taking in the cream of the walls and then the medical equipment around her, tracing the IV line from the bag to the back of her hand.

What did I do, she wondered? And just where am I? The last thing she remembered was desperately turning down a road, trying to lose the car that was tailing her. She didn't remember much after turning on to that road, where it led, she had no idea. She had felt the scrape and bang as her car had been sideswiped and, despite her best efforts, landed in the ditch. She had no memory of what had followed. Someone had come to her assistance, apparently, for her to be there.

She turned as she heard quiet footsteps approaching the bed and frowned at the older man who stood there, studying her, before he reached for her wrist and assessed her pulse.

"Now, young lady, how are you feeling?" Doc's eyes were kind, but shadowed, not knowing how she would react to Blair when he appeared.

Devaney shrugged, not quite sure if he was to be trusted. "Okay, I guess. Where am I?"

"In our local hospital. I know the police have been in. And I am told your car has been towed to a local garage." He watched her closely. "Where were you heading?"

She shrugged, wincing at the movement. "What did I do to myself?"

"Bumps. Bruises. You have a laceration on your shoulder, what from we're not sure. There are older bruises. You have some scars as well. From recent years, I would suspect." He shook his head as she refused to look at him. "You'll need a place to stay. I have spoken with my wife about a young lady I met who needs a home. She wants you to come stay with us."

"I can't do that! You don't know me!" She was shocked, but secretly pleased. Just maybe, she thought, I can find somewhere to hide and recover.

"Anna wants you to. She takes strays under her wing. You'll be able to leave in a while, once the IV is done. We'll make arrangements to get you to our home." He hesitated, then shook his head. Blair could explain, he thought. "We live in a building with a number of suites. You, in fact, were on the road to our place when you had the accident."

Devaney watched as he walked away before her head went back on the pillow and her eyes closed. Her head was aching and so was her heart. She wanted to see Blair, had in fact tracked him to this area, but she didn't know for sure where he was. She didn't want him to know she was here. He had been threatened years ago and that was part of the reason she had walked away. She was trying so hard to find the man or woman responsible for the threats against him and the accidents she herself had faced. But then, she did't know if she wanted to see him again, not after what she had done.

Devaney heard footsteps approaching her, heavier footsteps, she thought. A man's. Probably a police officer back to question her again. She hadn't told much. She couldn't. She had no proof who had been in the car. She had hoped that she had lost her pursuer, but wasn't sure. She didn't pray that she did. She no longer prayed, no longer trusted God like she had.

Blair stood by the side of Devaney's bed, his hands jammed into his jacket pockets, wanting to reach for her, but knowing he couldn't. Not yet. He wasn't sure if he ever would be able to.

Devaney sensed she knew the man standing there but refused to open her eyes. She didn't want to see Blair, if in fact that was him. She felt a hand rest on top of hers, the thumb circling near her own thumb. Then she felt a gentle hand brush down her hair before knuckles gently wiped at the tears she had not been aware she had cried. She heard the sound of the man's body as he turned slightly as other footsteps approached.

"Blair? Here's her knapsack. John brought it around for you. We'll be out in the waiting room when you're ready." Bradon's voice was quiet before his eyes searched the young lady's face. He nodded and turned away, not hearing Blair's soft words of thanks.

—

Blair turned back, his eyes on Devaney, before he sighed. She was not making it easy, and that was not the lady he remembered, the lady he loved.

"Devaney?"

His soft baritone voice washed through her mind, bringing back so many memories. She finally opened her eyes, to find him standing there, taller than she remembered, his hair cut somewhat shorter. She searched his face, seeing the lines time had started to work into it, the neatly trimmed beard and then she raised her eyes to his, finding his watchful, concerned, uncertain, caring, and full of the love he had always told her he had for her.

"Devaney? Talk to me, please? Why are you here? And just where have you been?" Blair waited, not sure how she would respond.

"Blair? You shouldn't be here. You shouldn't be around me." Devaney stared at him before she looked past him towards the door. "You need to leave."

"No, I'm not leaving. Not ever again. Not until you can explain to me fully and with the truth of why you walked away." Blair's hand tightened on hers, drawing her attention to that.

"I can't explain, Blair. I just can't." She refused to look up at him.

"Then, I'll take you to Doc and Anna's. You stay there, we'll talk." At his words, her eyes raised, startled. "Yes, I am friend's with Doc Elliott, who was just in here."

With that, he dropped her knapsack on the bed and turned and walked away, Devaney's mouth open as she watched him just that. He's never done that before, she thought.   What did I do to him?

Chapter 4

Keeping Devaney's hand tight his and her knapsack over one shoulder, Blair walked carefully towards Bradon's truck, where the two men waited for him, Branigan standing by the open doors, the sidewalks still icy and somewhat snow covered under the ice. Branigan searched Blair's face, seeing the shuttered look on it, before his gaze lowered to the lady beside Blair. So, this is the lady Blair loves. Lord, what do we do? How do we proceed?

Blair stood for a moment, his eyes on Bradon's truck, before Branigan spoke.

"Barnabas had Baird take your truck home."

"Thanks. I totally forgot about it until now." Blair grinned at his friend before he lifted Devaney into the truck and then slid onto the seat beside her. "Buckle up, Devaney."

She glared at him for a moment before she did that. She was confused, not knowing who the two men were that Blair seemed to know so well. She watched as best she could in the darkness of the night as Bradon drove away from town and then turned onto the same road she had taken.

Blair heard Devaney's breath be quickly indrawn and without thinking, reached for her hand, tightening his grip as she tried to pull away.

"This is the road you took, Devaney. It leads to The Barnabas Foundation. I work for that Foundation as do my two friends here." He watched her face in the dim light, seeing blankness on it. "Doc lives there as well. In fact, there are a number of us who are employed by the Foundation who work and live there."

Devaney felt the fear rising in her as she stared out the truck window, seeing where her car had dived into the ditch.

"Where did you find me?" She was certain Blair had been the one to find her.

"Brady found you off the road in the trees. He wouldn't let me near you. In fact, I didn't know it was you until they went to load you into the rig."

"You didn't?" She finally turned to him, her face lifted to study his. "Then, why?"

"Why? Why what, Dev?"

"Why were you there?" She was puzzled and not thinking straight, that much she knew. Time had taken a toll on her and she was exhausted, worn out in body and soul, her emotions shut down.

"Why? Because I was on my way home." He pointed ahead of them. "That's where I live." He shared a look with Branigan who had turned to study Devaney. "I couldn't not stop to help whoever it was. I don't think you realize just how your car was. It was nose down in the ditch. There is no way you could have gotten it out on your own. There was no sign of a driver. None of us could walk away and leave that person out there. We had no idea it was you. These two friends came looking for me at

Anna's request, given the weather. We searched as did the emergency personnel. Our friend, Brady, is a paramedic. He was the one who was on duty, the team called to the accident."

Bradon pulled to a stop in front of the Foundation building, watching with amusement as Devaney's head twisted as she stared at it, her eyes tracing up the building's three floors.

Devaney clamped her mouth closed. This was not what she had expected, not at all. She sat, even after Blair opened her door, and then reached to undo her seatbelt. She felt his hand on hers, tugging her from the truck and then leading her to the doors. She stopped inside the door, her mouth dropping open as her eyes roamed the lobby.

"Not what you expected?" Blair grinned, knowing how she was seeing it for the first time. There were seating areas on either side, with comfortable chairs and couches, a gas fireplace on opposite walls. The floors were hardwood, something Barnabas had insisted on. A security desk sat off to one side, near the corridor leading to the office complex.

She shook her head, even as he tugged at her hand and led her to the elevators. "Not at all. What kind of place is this?"

"It's the headquarters for The Barnabas Foundation." He waited, seeing her processing what he had told her.

"I've heard of that. But that doesn't explain why you're here."

"Because I am employed by the Foundation and have been since I finished college." He saw the sadness that briefly flickered across her face. "I looked for you before I came east. I tried so hard to find you, Devaney."

She didn't say anything, just finally giving a brief nod. "I had to leave, Blair." She watched as the doors slid open and he once more led her from the elevator.

"I need to stop at my suite, and then I'll take you to Anna." He unlocked his door, his hand to her lower back as he directed her inside. "Take a look around. Have a seat. I just need to change." His work boots hit the tray in the hall cupboard and his jacket a hanger before he walked away, Devaney watching him.

Blair stood a few minutes later, his eyes on Devaney who had not moved from where she had stood. He shook his head and moved towards her, startling her. He frowned as she cringed back from him. Lord, what has happened to her?

Chapter 5

Afraid to move, Devaney stood still, just letting her eyes roam what she could see of Blair's apartment. She liked the rustic colours tones he had chosen, knowing those were the colours that he liked: brown, rust, orange, with some cream thrown in. She heard his footsteps coming towards her and looked up, seeing the inscrutable look on his face and sighed to herself. At some point, they would need to talk, and she was not ready to do that at all.

She stared down at the work sock clad feet of Blair before her eyes raised once more to his, a frown on her face as his mouth opened and then closed, his head shaking as he did so.

Blair reached for shoes, slipping into them, before he reached to take her backpack, not saying a word, not knowing what to say. Lord, this is hard. What do we do? Where do we go? I still love her, always will, but I don't know how she feels towards me. Not any more.

He motioned to the door, pulling it closed behind him before he reached for her hand, his warm on hers, leading her towards the stairs.

"If it's okay, I'd like to walk you down. That way, you can get a feel for the building."

"And why would I want to do that? I'm not staying." She knew she sounded belligerent, not herself, not the lady he had known.

Blair shrugged. "If you don't, then you don't. I know Doc and Anna would like you to. If you have nowhere else, that is. If you do, once we can get back out, I'll take you there myself."

She stared up at him, tripping slightly as she took a step down, his hands out to catch her.

"We need to talk, Devaney. And soon. I'll grant you tonight or what's left of it. But then we talk." Blair stared down at her as they stopped outside Doc's door, a gravity about him that she didn't recognize.

Devaney finally nodded. "Okay. We do need to." Her voice was low enough that he barely heard her

Doc stood for a moment, watching the two, not sure if he should speak. Blair looked up and spotted him.

"Devaney, you met Doc in the hospital. He was the physician treating you. He is also a good friend of mine as is his wife, Anna. Come. In we go." He left her little choice but to enter, her eyes searching Doc's face before she heard a gentle voice.

"And this is your lady, Blair? She's beautiful. Come, my dear. You've been through a lot in the last few hours. Let's get you settled into our guest suite and then you can sleep."

Anna's warm voice and the arm she wrapped around Devaney brought tears to the younger woman's eyes, tears she had not felt in years. She simply nodded, letting Anna guide her to the teal and cream bedroom.

"There's an attached bath. Take a shower or a bath or simply crawl into bed. Doc said you were tiny. He was right. I left some new pyjamas we had gotten for a granddaughter who's about your size. Use them tonight. They're our gift to you." Anna searched the younger woman's face before she kissed her cheek and then left.

She stood outside the bedroom, a troubled look on her face and a troubled feeling in her heart. Blair, my boy, she thought. She's hurting and I don't know why. I'm not sure she'll tell us or even tell you. We need to cover her with prayer.

Doc had watched the two women walk away before he pointed to the kitchen, reaching for the coffee pot and pouring mugs of coffee for both himself and Blair. He knew Blair would not be sleeping, not yet at any rate.

"Blair? Care to talk?" Doc's voice was low as he settled himself at the table.

Blair shrugged. "I'm not sure what to say, Doc. I lost that lady so many years ago. To have her here, like this? I have no words." He looked up, a bleak look on his face. "I don't know her anymore, Doc. I'm not sure if she'll even want to stay with me."

"But she still wears your ring, doesn't she?"

Blair nodded. "She does, but it might just be out of habit."

Anna's arm came around his shoulders as she passed by him, stopping to hug him as she would her own son.

"I don't think so, Blair. I caught a look on her face when you weren't watching her, when she looked back down the hall. She still cares, but isn't sure what to do about it. It's been a lot of years."

"It has, Anna, and I'm not sure we can overcome what happened." Blair finally stood, swaying slightly, Doc on his feet, a hand on Blair's arm.

"Crash here, tonight, Blair. There's the other spare room. Or take the couch. It won't be the first time you've done that."

Chapter 6

Her hand on the closed door the next morning, Devaney hesitated to reach for the knob. She glanced down at the clothes Anna had left for her, jeans, a nice sweater, heavy socks. It had been years since she had had nice clothes, had been able to buy anything new. She shopped at thrift shops, buying with distaste what others had donated. She hated that attitude but she had had no choice. She sighed. Now, to face Blair. How did she do just that? She could tell he was hurt, was puzzled, but still wanted to hear her story. What could she tell him? She didn't want him near her. That, she thought, was why she had been run off the road. She had chosen the road to here, not realizing it led to Blair, but whoever was following her had known just that. Whoever it had been had chosen to run her off the road. She could have been killed or more seriously injured. She ached all over, she thought, not even the hot shower helping.

She stepped quietly down the hall, her eyes searching, not hearing many sounds, until she stopped in the kitchen doorway, Anna turning with a smile on her face.

"How did you sleep, Devaney? May I call you that?" Anna was across the kitchen, sweeping Devaney into a warm hug.

Devaney hesitated a moment before she hugged Anna back, tears prickling at her closed eyelids.

"I slept well. The best in a long time. But I shouldn't have slept so late." Devaney grimaced slightly from pain as she moved backwards.

"Doc said you'd be sore today. He left some medications for you." A frown crossed Anna's face as Devaney shook her head. "You need to, love. It's an over the counter one."

"I can't, Mrs. Elliott. I'm sorry. I've seen too many lives destroyed and lost."

"It's Anna, and it's okay. We'll get you better. Now, sit. Which do you prefer, coffee, tea, hot chocolate? If not those, we have water and juice."

Devaney remembered to shut her mouth. She had not had such a choice in years, she thought.

"Tea would be nice." She stood hesitating for a moment before she slid onto a chair, her hand coming out to feel the texture of the colourful placemats Anna had on the table, not seeing the compassionate look Anna was giving her.

Anna set a cup of tea in front of the younger woman and then paused, her hand in the air before she laid it on Devaney's head, feeling her flinch slightly. What has she been through, Lord? What does she need to heal from? We need our Buckley to talk to her. But will she talk to a minister? I get the sense that she has walked away from You. We need to bring her back.

Asked what she wanted to eat, Devaney had stared at Anna before she spluttered, her words not making sense. Anna had simply laughed and then reached for food, finally setting a plate of French toast and a bowl of fruit in front of her.

—

Devaney ate, her thoughts not on the food, but on Blair. She wouldn't ask where he was, knowing he would be at work. He was that conscientious. She shifted in her seat, uncomfortable at being inside for so long. She had lived on the streets for months, seeking a room when she had work to provide funds for that.

Her head turned as she heard the outside door open and then male voices and laughter in the hallway. She recognized Blair's as he protested in laughter at the teasing he was undergoing. She sighed. She did have to face him, but how? How did she tell him why she walked away all those years ago? How did she tell him about the threats against his life, the accusations she knew to be unfounded? She had tried so hard to find the one responsible, tracking that person across the country, always just a step or two behind them.

The three younger men and Doc spilled into the kitchen, the younger men greeting Anna with a hug and kiss before they looked over the food supplies she had left on the counter, knowing they would be in shortly. Blair gently moved Anna to one side, a grin on his face as he did so, a quiet comment that had her laughing at him, before he reached for the eggs and bread, soon plating French toast for the men.

Doc had drawn Anna to a side with a question before he nodded, heading for his office. Anna watched the bewilderment on Devaney's face before she took pity on her and sat beside her, an arm around her.

"They do this to me, Devaney. They walk in and take over, just like that." Anna watched the younger woman closely, seeing her nervousness and beginning agitation. A prayer rose for her.

Blair was watching Devaney as well, even as he worked away and joked with his two friends. Branigan's eyes moved between the young couple, a frown beginning on his face before he looked at the third man. Buckley Cullen, a close friend but also their minister, worked away side by side with Blair, a grin on his face as he accepted his fair share of teasing. Branigan placed the plates of food on the table as he was handed them, Buckley placing mugs of coffee and then startling Devaney as he set a fresh cup of tea in front of her, her eyes raising in fright before they shuttered.

Doc stood in the hallway where he could see but not be seen, his eyes on Blair, seeing the underlying tension in his friend before his eyes shifted to Devaney, a prayer rising from his heart as well, not sure where it was going but sensing Blair and Devaney were in danger, just as he had with Baird and Berneen and Benen and Cadee. Where does it end, Lord? Where does it end?

Chapter 7

His eyes watchful, Blair slid into the seat beside Devaney, catching her slight jump as he did so. He sighed. How did he get to know her once more? He had not stopped loving her, never would, even if she walked away. She would take his heart with her, he knew, if she did so. They needed to get to know one another again. He reached for her hand as Doc led them in a blessing on their food, her hand fisting and then relaxing under his. His eyes opening once more, he watched for the corner of an eye, seeing her restlessness and anxiety.

Laughter spiced the conversation over the meal, the younger men taking the teasing Doc and Anna directed their way. Devaney kept her head down, seeming to study her mug, but her eyes watched closely through her lashes. She didn't see the looks Blair shot her way, even as his conversations with his friends continued. She jumped as his hand reached for her plate as the younger men cleared the kitchen, food stuffs away in their proper place, dishes in the dishwasher, the counter and stove wiped off, the mugs of coffee refilled as was her mug of tea.

Blair settled himself once more beside Devaney, his arm along the back of her chair, not quite touching her. He didn't watch her face but felt her jump as he did that. His eyes were on Doc.

"Buckley? Will you pray for us?" Blair's voice caused Devaney to turn to search his face, not sure why he was asking that. "Devaney, Buckley's a good friend. He is also our pastor."

Devaney stared at him and then at Buckley, gathering herself to push her chair backwards, unable to do so as Blair's arm laid across it. She felt trapped, unable to escape, and that was a feeling she hated. She had been trapped too many times over the last few years, just escaping death or a physical assault.

Buckley's head was down as he prayed, leading them to the throne of God, his words as simple as a child talking to his beloved Father, but deep enough that they were challenged. His heart broke for his friend, knowing the conflict he was undergoing. These two had had a brief moment to speak earlier that day.

Doc studied the four younger people, his eyes lingering on Blair and then Devaney, seeing her discomfort at being in close contact with them. *What has she been through, Lord, that has led to this?*

Devaney listened to the conversation that started after the prayer, not wanting to be there, not wanting to take part.

"Devaney?" Blair's voice was close to her ear. "Talk to us. Tell us why you were running."

She shook her head, not looking up, not wanting to see the anger and censure she was sure would be on their faces.

"Devaney? Please? Look at me." When she refused, his hand came out and gently turned her face to him. "Devaney, you will look at me and now." His words lashed at her, not in anger, but with concern.

Her eyelashes raised and she studied him, seeing the man she had fallen in love with, his care, concern, compassion and love on his face.

"I can't." Her voice was barely a whisper.

"You can, but you won't. So, how be I take a guess at it? Remember, I know you well enough to read your face, even if you try to hide the truth." He waited, and then sighed, his eyes searching the ones sitting, waiting for her to speak.

"Devaney, I don't know exactly why you ran, but it was something big that made you do that. Someone you loved was threatened. It had to be me. You wouldn't have taken that step if it had been another friend or our foster family. What was I threatened with? Assault? Injury? Death? Loss of my good name? How close am I to the truth?"

Tears sparkled on her eyelashes as she first shook her head and then her face was buried in her folded arms on the table as silent sobs shook her body. Blair's arm was around her, his head bent close to hers as he whispered gently and then began to pray, pray as he never had before. His lady was hurting and he just wanted to make her better.

The other four watched silently before Buckley rose and came around the table, his hands reaching to lay softly on Blair's head and Devaney's as well. His prayer filled the room, stopping Devaney's sobs as she listened.

Blair finally raised her head once more, his eyes on her face as she refused to look at him.

"Devaney, please. Talk to us. No one blames you, least of all me. I, we, just want to help you. To help you find whoever it is that did this to you."

She finally nodded, her eyes on Branigan, a frown on her face. "I know you."

Branigan frowned, a puzzled look on his face. "We met last night."

"No." She shook her head. "I know you. Not from here."

Branigan shook his head again, and then paused. "Regina. You were in Regina. Your backpack had been stolen and I returned it to you. I never got your name, you were gone so quickly."

Devaney nodded. "Thank you. You were so kind. You made sure I was okay but I couldn't stay. He was watching me. He would have hurt you if I had stayed."

"Who would have hurt you, Devaney?" Branigan began to push, his employment as a security systems specialist coming to the forefront.

"I don't know his name. He was around before we finished college, Blair. I would find him watching you and then me. I found letters I think came from him, warning me against you. Telling me you were no good. That you were into crime. I knew he was wrong. I knew it because I knew you." Her voice shook with her emotions but her face remained shuttered.

"Devaney. Oh, why didn't you come to me or to our foster father?" Blair's heart hurt for his lady.

—

"I couldn't, Blair. The last photo I got was of you, walking towards me, but you had a red X through you." She stared at him. "He would have killed you, right then and there. I know he would have."

Chapter 8

They had finally stood, the six of them, Devaney almost running to the bedroom she had used, the door closing quietly behind her. She sank to the floor by the bed, unable to weep, unable to think, just unable to do anything. She couldn't pray. She had tried so hard the first year or so, to pray, to ask for guidance, for protection, but God didn't seem to hear or answer her. She rubbed at her shoulder, at the scar from the knife attack that first year she was on the run. They told her she was lucky, the medical people she had seen, that it could have killed her. She just didn't understand why God hadn't stopped it.

Blair stood in the hallway, his eyes on her closed door, his thoughts muddled. He didn't know which way to turn, which way to think, or what to do. This had not been what he had expected to hear. His thoughts raised in prayer, he turned as he felt a hand on his shoulder. Branigan stood there, a frown of concern on his face.

"Blair? What are you thinking?" Branigan's voice was low, covered by the sounds of the conversation in the kitchen.

Blair shrugged. "To tell you the truth, Branigan? I don't know. I never dreamed that was why she had disappeared. I mean, I thought she had a line on her family and was trying to trace it, without worrying me. That's what I thought the note meant." His eyes grew more troubled, his heart heavier, his thoughts darker. "I wish she had spoken to me. I would have helped her."

"She didn't but we can now. Let me have all the information you can think of. Our guys will work on it. Talk to your foster mother, see what she has to say." Branigan's body shifted as he heard footsteps behind him, and Buckley appeared. "Buckley?"

Buckley's look of concern stopped their words. "Blair? How strong a Christian was she?"

"One of the strongest I've known. She had a rough life, shifted from home to home until she was about 12. That's when she ended up in the home I was in. Our foster parents were strong Christians and that helped her. But, now?" He shook his head, his eyes back on the door down the hall. "She tried to run when you went to pray. She's not open to God any more."

"No, she's not. She feels abandoned by Him. We'll pray that she finds her way back and soon." Buckley's hand rested lightly on Blair's shoulder before he excused himself and walked away, heading for the church office and the sermon he was working on for Sunday. He frowned as he did so, knowing that he had just changed his sermon. He paused, staring at the iciness the storm was still spreading and sighed. Guess I'm not going that way, am I, Lord? He turned as he heard footsteps heading his way and waited for Brady to catch up with him.

"Buckley? How's Blair? Have you seen him today?" Brady's voice held his concern for his friend.

"I did. We just had breakfast with Doc and Anna. Branigan's heading down to his office to do

---

some research." Buckley paused and then motioned for Brady to go with him. "Come with me, Brady. We need to talk."

Brady sank into a chair in Buckley's office, not sure what to expect. He watched his friend closely, seeing how disturbed he was.

"Buckley? What can you share?" Brady waited, knowing Buckley would speak when he could and share what he was able to.

"Brady, it's bad. She's been on the run, trying to protect Blair. She's moved across the country, town by town, city by city. She doesn't know who, only that Blair was threatened. She admitted to Blair that just when they were graduating, she received a photo with an "X" through him. She felt she had no choice." Buckley stopped, unable to comprehend how she must have felt.

"And Blair feels guilty. He would. He would have asked her to let him help her, but she didn't or wouldn't or couldn't."

Buckley nodded. "That's how I imagine he is. He hasn't said, won't say. He wants to make it all better for her and can't. He's not even sure if she'll stay with him or move on. If she moves on, she'll take his heart with him."

"I thought that last night. I didn't know what to do, what to expect, when he said that. It's not what I thought he would say."

"None of us did. It caught all of us off guard. With Baird and Benen going through what they have, we didn't want anyone else to have that experience." Buckley sat back, rubbing at his face, fatigue

43

weighing him down. He had not slept the night before, not when he heard what had happened. He had been that burdened for his friend.

"Now what?" Brady sat forward, reaching for a pad of paper and a pen. He liked to make notes, needed them to help organize his thoughts.

"Now what? We pray. I think she'll try and run again, just to keep Blair safe. He said she wanted to run when I prayed. His arm around her was the only thing that kept her in her chair."

"Okay. Number one - pray for her to come back to God. Number two - pray for this guy, whoever he is, to be caught and caught quickly. Next?" Brady looked up, a frown on his face as Buckley didn't respond. "Buckley?"

Buckley looked up, his eyes narrowed before he shook his head, clearing his thoughts, the frown on his face disappearing. "She had met Branigan."

"Last night. I know she did." Brady continued to frown, his eyes watchful. "What?"

Buckley was shaking his head. "No. She had met him before. She questioned him. Branigan remembered that he had run into her in Regina, that her backpack had been stolen and he returned it to her." Buckley paused, a frown gathering once more on his face. "She said if she had stayed, Branigan would have been hurt."

"So, whoever this guy is, he's staying very close to her. She's afraid to get close to anyone, to ask anyone for help."

"We need to keep her here. At least in the building, if not on the property." Brady's head went back as his eyes slid closed. "Not that it matters. They managed to get to Berneen and Cadee both here on the property." Brady had mentioned Baird's Berneen and Benen's Cadee, who had been endangered on the very property.

"That's my fear. I'm sure it's Blair's as well. He can't stay with her, not like Baird and Benen." Buckley sighed. "But I can see him wanting to take that step, to marry her, just to keep her close to him."

Brady nodded, his head turning as he heard a knock at the door. "I can see that as well."

Chapter 9

Cracking open the door, Breck peered in and then entered, the door closely behind him. His eyes searched Buckley's face before he sat, not saying a word, his thoughts muddled for once.

"Breck?" Brady's voice finally cut through his thoughts.

"Buckley? How's Blair?"

Buckley grinned. "Brady just asked me that not too long ago." He sobered. "He's hurting, Breck. For himself. For his lady. He's not sure where to turn or what to do."

Breck nodded. "I gathered that. How do we help him?"

"Prayer. Support." Buckley sighed. "He's not sure what he wants to do. He's waiting for Devaney to speak with him, and she's not. She's shut down and has been for a while." Buckley exchanged a glance with Brady, not sure what was going on with Breck. He was distracted, that much was obvious.

Breck was on his feet, pacing, before he turned, mouth open to speak, then shook his head and walked out of the office, leaving the two men staring after him.

"Did he just do that?" Brady stared at the closed door.

"He did. He wanted something but wasn't sure how to express it." Buckley studied his desk for a moment. "Pass the word, will you, Brady? Church is cancelled tomorrow. We'll meet here somewhere instead."

Brady nodded as he stood, his eyes on his fingers he was rubbing together. "What about Blair?"

Buckley sighed, sitting back in his chair, his eyes on Brady. "We'll have to leave that with God. There's not much we can do. The police will be investigating. Devaney isn't open to our meddling as Anna would say. Blair is quiet, too quiet."

Brady frowned, then grimaced. "I don't like it, Buckley. Not after what Baird and Benen went through. I don't want to see another one of us go through that."

Buckley nodded again. "And that's exactly what I think will happen."

Brady stood watching Baird, Benen, Bradon and Branigan as they talked in the lobby before he walked towards them, their circle opening up to include him.

"Brady?" Branigan shot a glance at the stairs.

Brady shrugged, a puzzled look on his face. "I don't get it, Branigan. How did she remember you?"

Branigan stared at him. "I don't know. I need to talk to her again, but I don't think she'll say more than she has." He turned as he heard footsteps approaching. "Blair?"

Blair just shook his head as he stopped. "Don't ask me, Branigan. I don't know how she remembered

you. She always has been able to do that. It's scary."
He looked around at his friends, knowing the other
six of their friends were around the building
somewhere. "Church tomorrow?"

"It's here." Brady looked around as well.
"Will Devaney be with you?"

Blair shrugged, a puzzled look crossing his face
for a moment. "I have no idea. I pray she is, but I
can't guarantee anything." He paused and then
turned and walked away, to stand at the front doors,
staring out, leaving his friends to exchange glances.

Baird followed him. "Blair?"

Blair hesitated and then turned to Baird. "How
did you ever do it, Baird?"

Baird shrugged. "I'm not sure I could even tell
you other than God saw us through."

Blair nodded. "I know that. It's a given He
does that. But emotionally, how did you manage?"

"It was tough, Blair. It was different for us.
We were married, even though we didn't know one
another. That was tough."

"I get that, Baird. I just don't know how you
kept your head or your faith."

"Prayer from my friends. You all supported us.
It was difficult and at times I really doubted." Baird
stopped for a moment, gathering his thoughts. "Now,
about you and Devaney."

Blair shrugged. "I am not sure there is an us
any more, Baird. I can't reach her, and I should be
able to." He paused and then walked away, heading

---

for the small chapel Barnabas had installed in the building, knowing that was where he needed to be. Please, God, bring her back to me. If not, please remove the love I have for her. I can't go on, not knowing, not loving her like I am and do.

Chapter 10

Her arms wrapped around herself, Devaney stood the next morning in the small chapel, her eyes searching for something, anything. She did not want to be there, that was a given, she thought, but she felt she had too. Anna had asked if she was coming, taking for granted that she was. She felt a hand touch her back and shifted to look at who it was. Blair, of course, she thought. She was trying to avoid him but given the close quarters they were in at the moment, that didn't seem possible.

Blair watched the shuttered look on Devaney's face and sighed. This was not her, he thought. She was always so open, so interested in those around her. How do we get her back to that, Lord? He hesitated for a moment and then nudged her to a seat in the back row, sitting beside her. He caught the curious and compassionate looks of his friends before he saw Cadee and Benen sit beside them.

Devaney jumped as she felt a hand touch her arm. Carefully schooling her emotions, she looked to the side, a frown on her face for a moment. What had she walked into, she wondered?

Cadee waited for a moment before her eyes raised to Blair, whose own eyes were on Devaney, not realizing his emotions were out there for everyone else to read.

"This is Cadee Carroll, Devaney. And that's her husband, Benen, beside her. They have had an adventure that they need to tell you about." Blair waited for a reaction from Devaney, a frown once more on his face as she just quietly said hi and then shifted her glance to the front of the chapel.

Cadee shared a glance with Benen before she looked up at Blair, shaking her head.

"Devaney, would you like to join us for lunch?" Cadee's voice was soft, a question in it that Blair had never heard before.

Devaney's gaze shifted to her and then she turned to look at Blair. He waited, letting her make her own decision, knowing he would back her, to some extent, whatever it was. She finally nodded, thinking it was easiest just to go and then she could leave. She prayed, as much as she did now, that the weather would be clear enough on the following day that she could leave. She didn't want to be there. Didn't want to be the one bringing danger to Blair or his friends and that she knew was a real possibility.

Buckley's voice caught her attention and she frowned once more as she studied him. Her head tilted as she did so, catching Blair's attention. This was not a man who she thought would be a minister. Just how did he fit in here? She studied all the other men, catching sight of another young woman around her own age, sitting beside Anna. She had heard Doc had made his way back into town, just how, she wasn't sure.

Buckley's eyes found Blair's, who nodded. He sighed to himself even as he led the hymns and choruses he had chosen for that day, Burney at the piano, Breck on guitar to accompany them.

He paused before he stared his message, his thoughts muddled, fear for his friend and his lady uppermost in his mind. Lord, I have no idea what to say. I have printed words in front of me but they just don't seem to fit today. Lead here, Lord. Please?

Buckley's hand reached for his papers and he literally tossed them over his shoulders, bringing a quick laugh from his friends, and a deeper frown from Devaney.

"Sorry, folks. I had a message planned. Not what God wants this morning." He moved to stand and lean on the pulpit. "God is here. He is always here. Now, this morning, we share. We pray. We talk. God had isolated us at this time because of the weather. We can't be isolated from one another." He looked around, seeing the understanding on the faces, his focus on Devaney's, not quite sure what was going on with her.

Barnabas began to pray, his voice echoing through the chapel, leading them to the throne of God. Other voices picked up. Devaney jumped as Blair's hand covered hers and she glanced up at him, seeing his eyes on her, reading in them his love for her, before his voice picked up the chain and he prayed for them all, and for whatever situation they found themselves in.

Devaney stood at the end of the time, her head already shifting away from what she had heard, but her heart had listened. It had started to crack the hardness she had developed over time. She followed Blair as he walked away, his hand on hers. She hesitated about that, but then shrugged. She would allow him that today. Tomorrow, she would be gone, once more. She couldn't stay near him. She just couldn't.

Chapter 11

The weather had warmed up enough by the Monday morning that the ice had melted. Blair stood outside, his eyes on Devaney as she paced in front of him. She's going to run, he thought, and how do I see her from doing just that, Lord? I need to keep her safe, but I'm not sure she'll let me do just that. He walked towards her, finding her backing away from him.

"Blair?" She had a question in her voice, trying desperately not to let him see she wanted him to stop her from moving but knowing she had to stay away from him.

"Devaney? I won't let you run. Not again. We need to talk. We need to decide where we go."

She shook her head even as his hand on her arm stopped her movement. "We have nowhere to go, Blair. You need to stay away from me."

"I won't, my love. I just won't." He turned as he heard the sound of a motor revving and heard Devaney's scream, even as he reached to pull her towards him and then towards the other side of the parking lot, the truck heading for them at a higher speed that was usually seen. He could hear shouts from his friends but as he glanced over his shoulder and saw the truck looming behind them, he knew he would not make it in time. He wrapped Devaney in his arms and threw himself to one side, the truck

---

fender glancing off him before it spun and sped away, mission accomplished.

Blair landed in a heap beside his truck and lay still, Devaney still in his arms. He didn't hear the shouts of the men as they ran towards him, Doc reaching him first. Hands reached to gently move Devaney away even as Doc's hands reached for Blair, feeling for a pulse, a moment of stillness as he found it, before he looked over at Devaney.

"Is she alive?" His words cut through the stillness.

"She is, Doc." Breck was on his knees beside her as was Branigan. "She is. Blair?"

"I don't know." He looked around. "The backboards and collars, guys. We need to get them out of here." He turned back to Blair, even as he heard sirens rising and falling in the distance and getting closer. "Never mind. Help is here."

The men stood back, watching as the two were worked on and then loaded into the ambulances, the red and blue lights of the emergency vehicles flickering across their faces. Barnabas had picked two of the men to go with Blair and Devaney, just staring down the paramedics until they nodded. He was afraid for Blair, afraid that he would not survive. He had read the look on Doc's face.

Berneen and Cadee had ran for Anna and then for one of their vehicles, following after the ambulances, knowing someone had to be there for their friends. Anna's face was taut, knowing from the look on Doc's face just how worried he was.

—

Barnabas turned as a patrol officer approached him.

"Barnabas? What happened?" Frank Wills looked around, a frown on his face as he watched the team of officers reconstructing as best they could what had happened.

"I'm not sure, Frank. I was in my office and Breck pulled me out here. I can't tell you who was around, but some of them were. That I know."

"Okay. Let me talk to them and see who knows what happened." Frank paused, then spoke again. "Who is the lady?"

"Devaney Daubney." Barnabas paused. "She was in an accident on Friday night, on our road. We found out at that time that she and Blair were engaged. I am not sure where that stands now."

Frank stared at him, knowing Blair from the garage he worked at. "Blair? Your Blair? Engaged?"

Barnabas nodded, even as he pulled his keys from his pocket, and stared at them. "I know. He never ever said. I'm not sure he ever would." He looked up, squinting in the sudden shaft of sunlight hitting his face. "If you don't need me any further, I'm off.'

"No, go ahead, Barnabas. I'll catch up with you. I will make sure Will knows where you are." He referenced the police chief, a good friend of Barnabas.

"Thanks, Frank. Let me know if you need anything further from me."

Barnabas stood an hour later, staring down at Blair as he lay on the hospital bed in the Emergency Department of their local hospital. He could see the scrapes and cuts and bruises that were already forming on his friend's arms and face. Why, Lord? Why Blair? Who did Devaney bring around him that endangered him? Who is after her, Lord? We need to find out and I am not sure she can even tell us.

He turned as he heard footsteps behind him. Doc stood there, his eyes on Barnabas before he walked to the end of the bed and studied Blair.

"Doc?" Barnabas was almost afraid to ask how Blair was.

"Barnabas, it's not pretty. He took a good hit from the truck. They'll be along shortly to take him for imaging but his lower right leg is broken. How bad yet, we don't know. I have an orthopaedic surgeon heading this way. Internal injuries we are still assessing. What was he thinking?"

"Thinking of saving Devaney more than likely." Barnabas turned to stare at the door behind him. "Who's with her?"

"Anna. We have no next of kin listed for her. She's been in the province long enough to register for insurance but she has nothing to say who to contact. Did Blair say anything?"

Barnabas shook his head. "No, he didn't but then we never really had a chance to talk. This has been such a surprise for us."

"That's what we thought. For now, I've talked to the Administration here. We are listing Blair and then Anna and myself or you for her. We need to do this. Someone has to take care of her."

"That's good." He turned once more, to study his friend and employee. "I'm going to track down Anna then." He stopped as Doc's hand came out to rest on his arm. "Doc?"

"Go find Devaney. She's in the room next door. She's still unconscious but she needs someone there."

Barnabas studied his friend. "What aren't you saying, Doc?"

Doc just shook his head. "Nothing. It's just a burden I have for her. Just like with Berneen and Cadee. These two are finished with what's going on. Not by a long shot."

Chapter 12

A hand to her head, Devaney groaned as her eyes flickered open and closed. Where are I am, she questioned, and why do I hurt so much? What did I go and do now? She jumped as she felt a hand gently move her own hand back down.

Her eyes opening, she stared around, fear in her heart, at the hospital room she found herself in. I can't do this, Lord. I just can't do this again. What did he do now? Her eyes sought the person she could hear with her and frowned. Do I know you, she wondered?

"Devaney, dear, you are awake." Anna watched as Devaney frowned. "I know it's confusing but we have met. Just a couple of days ago. I am Anna, a friend of Blair's."

"I'm sorry. Blair? I haven't seen him in years." Devaney was confused.

"But you have, dear. You've seen him every day for the last three days. Don't you remember?"

Devaney shook her head and then her eyes closed as the pounding intensified in it. "I'm sorry."

"Don't be. Doc said you likely wouldn't remember. That's okay. We'll get you two back together soon."

"No, I can't. I can't see him." Devaney was becoming more agitated by the second, leading to a frown crossing Barnabas' face as he had entered the room.

"Devaney? Who is after you?" Barnabas' voice broke through her agitation and her eyes flew to him in fright. "I'm Barnabas. I employ Blair."

"You do? Where is he?" She looked past Barnabas towards the door. "I don't believe you that he's here. I want to see him."

Barnabas' hand on her shoulder kept her in place, a frown shared with Anna at her words.

"You can't. Not right now. He's in surgery."

"Surgery?" Devaney sat upright, shoving Barnabas' hand to one side. "Why? What did he do to him?"

"Who? Who did this, Devaney? Do you know?"

"I don't know who. I don't know his name. He's been following me for years." She looked up, fear in her eyes. "Please? Will you help me? No one else will. I can't let Blair be hurt."

Anna's arms came around the younger woman. "Talk to us, Devaney. We'll help you, but you need to let us know what you know."

Devaney nodded, a yawn catching her unawares before her eyes closed and she slept once more. Anna glanced up at Barnabas, catching his eye and shaking her head.

"We won't get anything more from her for a while." Anna sighed, her eyes back on the younger woman. "Who did she mean?"

Barnabas shrugged. "I have no idea. Blair has never talked about her, not until now, and even now, he has not said much." He shrugged, his eyes on Devaney. "We'll have to wait, I guess. I know Will wants to speak with them both."

"I'm sure he does." Anna walked around the bed to hug Barnabas. "I fear for these two, that they are just beginning something that has no end, at least not for a while."

Barnabas finally walked away, heading for the surgical waiting room, finding his men wandering the hallway, waiting for word on Blair that hadn't come yet. He sighed. Another one like Baird and Benen, he thought, and then had the horrible thought that maybe just all of them would go through something similar. He prayed they didn't.

Chapter 13

Blair stirred in the early morning hours, not quite sure where he was. Blinking, he tried to focus, staring around, his eyes finally settling on the cast on his leg. He frowned, not remembering having done anything to cause a cast to be placed. He reached for it, feeling the tug on his hand and then frowned at the IV that ran to his hand. His other hand felt at his head, finding a bandage on the side of it. He hurt all over, he thought, not quite sure what had happened. He shifted in the bed, squinting at the door before he reached for the IV and pulled it, a hand clamped over the spot for a moment, before he shoved at the blankets and pulled himself from the bed and then headed for the cupboard, knowing he'd find his clothes there.

It was awkward, he decided, to dress, balancing on the cast as he did so. He turned towards the door, finding Branigan standing there, a smile on his face.

"Breaking out, are you, Blair?"

Blair gave a grim nod. "I need to find Devaney. That was deliberate."

Branigan's hand came out to help steady Blair. "Here. Use your crutches. You do realize it's only four in the morning?"

"It is? Doesn't matter. Let's leave." Blair stared at Branigan's hand on his arm before his eyes raised and he searched his friend's face. "Branigan?"

—

"She's here in the hospital as well. You two were run down yesterday. You can't leave without permission, Blair."

Blair looked past him at Doc. "Doc's here. Is he my doctor?"

Doc just shook his head and handed over papers to him. "We figured you'd do this. Baird is waiting downstairs. Your lady is next door. Berneen is in with her, helping her get ready. We've all agreed to let you leave earlier than we should." He shook a finger at the younger man. "I'll put you in the infirmary if I have to, both of you, Blair. For now, Anna is waiting at home for you two. And no, you are not on your own for a few days. If you insist on that, you'll not leave here."

Blair's gaze flickered between the two men before he nodded. "I can do that. Now, find Devaney for me."

Doc watched him closed as he wielded his crutches and then shook his head. "He's not giving up on her, is he?"

Branigan shook his own head. "Not one bit, Doc. I am afraid for him. I talked to Barnabas earlier. He said that Devaney didn't believe that she had seen him in the last few days and that someone was after Blair. She doesn't want to be around him because whoever it is has threatened to kill him. She doesn't know why."

Doc's hand rested briefly on Branigan's shoulder. "He's hurting, Branigan. Hurting physically and then in any other way you could think of. His lady's back near him but doesn't want to be around him. That's something he doesn't understand. I'm not sure I even do."

"I'm not sure she'll stay or even let us know what is going on. I pray she does. Yesterday was too scary and too close for Blair." Branigan stared down at the floor, searching for what he wasn't sure.

"He won't let her away from him. Not this time." Doc nodded towards Devaney's door. "Go on, Branigan. Get them home."

Blair studied Devaney for a moment before his eyes raised to Berneen. "She's sleeping?"

Berneen nodded. "She could barely stay awake to let me help her dress. There is more going on with her, Blair, I fear, than just this."

Blair nodded, his eyes on Devaney. "I know there is, Berneen. Thank you." He looked around as the door opened and Branigan entered. "Are we set?"

Branigan stoped for a moment, his eyes on Devaney, before he reached to scoop her into his arms. "We are. Let's get you two out of here."

Blair slid onto the truck seat beside Devaney, his eyes on her as he clipped his seatbelt on and then reached to cradle her close to him, hearing her faint sigh as she turned her face to him. Branigan watched, a frown on his face, not sure what was going on. His eyes rested on Blair's face, seeing the worry, concern but something else there. Blair's thinking through this, he thought. We need to sit down with him and work through it.

Chapter 14

Blair stood in the doorway to Doc and Anna's living room, hands jammed into the sweatpants pockets he was wearing, the only thing he had that fit over the cast on his leg, crutches balanced under his arms. His eyes were on Devaney as she slept, fatigue and pain evident on her face. He turned his head slightly as he heard the outside door open and close and then felt a hand on his shoulder as Doc stood beside him.

"Has she awakened at all?"

Blair shook his head. "Not since we got her here. Berneen had trouble keeping her awake to get ready to leave the hospital." A frown covered his face. "Doc, what else is going on with her?"

Doc's face showed the compassion he felt at that moment, as he drew Blair to the kitchen and made him sit, reaching to prepare food for himself and then coffee for the both. He sat himself down, sighing as he did so. The last few days had been stressful in the Emergency Department and he had been on call to the local shelter as well.

"Doc?" Blair's voice was quiet, and when Doc didn't respond at first, he shifted in his chair to stare at the door.

"Blair, we need to talk, but let me eat first. It's been a long day." Doc watched Blair carefully, seeing underneath to where he was trying hard to stay strong, to trust in God, but knowing that his friend was suffering and doubting and struggling.

Blair nodded, knowing that Doc was right. He sighed to himself, his mind wandering back to when Devaney had walked away from him, just leaving him standing watching her, before he ran after her, a hand on her arm stopping her. She had refused to look at him, had stared straight ahead of her, a shuttered look similar to what she now wore on her face. His pleas and questions had not brought any further information from her. She had finally just moved away, almost on a run. He had run after her but she had disappeared. He had searched, had almost haunted her apartment complex but he couldn't find her. Friends had told him she was still in town, but when he went to the locations she was to be at, she wasn't. He had finally had to leave and take his work with The Barnabas Foundation. He had travelled back to the town a few times, searching for her, but never finding her. He had finally had to lay that burden down at the foot of God's throne.

Now, he wondered, where do I go with her? Lord, I just don't know. I still love her so much but I can't read her. Not like I used to. And I don't want to let her go, not if I can help it.

Doc sat when he finished his meal, his heart raised in prayer for his young friend and his lady, watching the conflicting emotions crossing Blair's face without him knowing that was happening.

"Blair?" Doc's voice finally reached through to him and he looked quickly at the older man. "Blair, let's pray. Then we'll talk."

Blair nodded, his head bowing as he listened to Doc pray, before he raised his head again, his eyes on his mug of coffee.

"Blair? Talk to me. Tell me if she had any health issues that you know of." Doc knew something was going on with Devaney, he wasn't sure what.

"She didn't have any, Doc. Unless she has developed something in the last few years. She was always so healthy." Blair looked up, his eyes on the wall across from him. "What is it you are asking me?"

"We ran some blood work. It came back mostly normal. But there are some factors I need to talk to her about. I was just trying to see if it was longstanding."

"Is it serious, Doc? Do I need to worry?" Blair's eyes held his concern even as he tried to focus on what Doc was saying or rather what he was not saying.

Doc shook his head. "No, it's not. But I need to talk to her first." He looked around as he heard a sound and Devaney appeared in the doorway. "Devaney, come and sit, my dear. Let me get you something to eat."

Devaney gave a brief nod as she sat, her eyes not quite staying open all the way. "Just some water please."

"No, Devaney. You will eat more than that." Doc's voice was firm. He set a glass of juice in front of her and then reached for the pot of soup on the stove, ladling some into a bowl he also set before her.

"Eat, or I'll take you downstairs to the infirmary and hook you up to an IV. Your choice."

Devaney looked up at him, assessing whether he really would do that, and then picked up her spoon, eating about half of what he had given her before she pushed the bowl away.

"You wanted to talk to me?" Devaney refused to look back up, knowing what he would have to say.

"I do. Do you need Blair to leave?" His kindly compassionate gaze rested on her, Blair's quiet shift in his chair caught on the periphery of his vision.

She shrugged. "I know what you are going to say. Those values, the hemoglobin ones, have been low but likely rising. I have been on iron, or at least I was. I ran out and couldn't get any more."

Doc shook his head. "You need to take that, Devaney. If you can't afford it, we'll look after it for you."

She abruptly shoved away from the table and headed for the bedroom she had used. She sank to the bed, arms wrapped around herself. How did she do this? How did she keep track of Blair but stay away from him? Her gaze on the door, she shuddered, knowing that whatever danger she had been facing on her own just became the danger Blair would face. She didn't want that for him. She wanted him to stay safe and he just wouldn't. He wouldn't stay away from her. Somehow, she needed to make that break and she knew it wouldn't happen. Her eyes on the ceiling, she sighed. Is this it, God? Is this how it ends? How do I find my way back to You? I can't do it on my own. She sat in silence, finding and feeling the peace she had not had for months, no, years, she thought. Thank you, God. Keep my Blair safe, that's all I ask.

Chapter 15

Blair watched her walk away and then looked at Doc, a question on his face.

"Doc? How do we do this?"

Doc sighed, rubbing at his head. "We don't, Blair. We can't force her to do anything. She's free to do what she wants. She can even walk away from us and we can't stop her." His hand came up at the protest Blair voiced. "I know, Blair. You're engaged to her, but you haven't seen her in so many years. To her, you're a stranger. And the same for you. You don't know her anymore. You need to let her have her freedom and space. Get to know her again. God has brought her here. It may be you'll stay a couple and marry. It may be that she'll give back your ring and move on."

Blair buried his face in his hands, prayers rising from within him. He finally looked up and towards the hall, knowing that Doc had spoken the truth.

"I know, Doc. That scares me. I don't want to lose her again, not if I can help it." He finally rose from the table, hesitated, and then walked from the apartment, his crutches thudding as he did so. He knew he needed to give her space, he just didn't want to.

He stood in the lobby, staring out the windows, watching as the warming weather had drips coming from the eaves-trough on the building and creating puddles on the pavement. His thoughts were muddled.   He could see no clear answers to the questions racing through his brain.

Bradon stood for a moment, Kade by his side, watching before he approached him.

"Blair?" When Blair didn't respond, he reached to touch his arm, causing Blair to shake his head and turn slightly. "What can we do for you? We are praying for you and Devaney. But, right now, what can we do?"

Blair finally turned to face him. "To tell you the truth, Bradon? I have no idea." His hand reached to rub at Kade's ears as the dog leaned into him. "I don't know. I know she'll try and run again. And I don't know if I can stop her, or even if I have the heart to."

"God knows, Blair. I know. It sounds like a repeated soft answer that doesn't convince or calm us of knowing that God is in control. But He is. He has placed you and she where you need to be right now." Bradon looked around, a frown on his face before it cleared. Devaney stood nearby, a questioning look on her face even as Kade moved to stand beside her, his nose nudging at her hand.

Devaney's eyes were on Blair, a question deep in them. She sighed to herself. She needed to walk away from him, but knew he would not let her. She wanted him to stay safe. Her hand rubbed at Kade, not even aware of what she was doing, before she walked forward, Kade keeping step with her, his eyes on her face. She stopped just short of Blair, knowing she needed to speak but hesitant to do that.

Blair watched her reflection in the window, not sure how to approach her. *This is not me, Lord. I should know how to talk to her, but I don't. Not anymore. She has had experiences she can't or won't talk about. She had them on her own, without me. I can't share that part of her life.* He finally turned to study her, finding her eyes showing her hurt and pain and something he just wasn't sure of. Her face was as shuttered as she could make it.

"Devaney?"

"Blair, you need to be sitting. Please?" Her voice held a plea for him to understand, but understand what he wasn't sure of either.

"Devaney, here you sit as well." He waited for her to slide down on the couch in front of one of the fireplaces in the lobby before he sat on the other end, motioning for Bradon to stay. Kade crowded close to Devaney, knowing there was something going on with her and wanting to bring comfort to her. Her hand rested on him.

Devaney had kept her eyes on Blair, not even seeing Bradon as he sat in one of the armchairs just out of her range of vision.

"Blair? You need to stay away from me."

"No, Devaney. Not anymore. It doesn't work that way. I have no idea what you have gone through, but God does. Whether you believe it or not, He is in control and has allowed this." His hand reached for hers, feeling the roughness of her skin, and sighed to himself. "How do I get through to you? I'm not running away from you. If you run, I will come after you. We need to talk, but I don't think you are ready for that."

She shook her head. "I'm not. Not yet. Maybe soon." She sighed, her head going back as she looked up before her eyes came back to meet his. "I'm not the same person I was, Blair. I've changed. I don't like who I have had to become to survive."

"I realize that, Devaney. Neither am I. We are not the people we were back then." He paused, his eyes on the dark hardwood floor, tracing the lines in the wood. "What I need to know is what happened to you all those years ago, who it was."

She shook for a moment, her eyes closing, her face turning white. "I can try, Blair, but it is not pretty."

"It never is. I get that, Devaney. We need to do this though. I, no we, need to be able to tell the police here what you went through and who caused it." His eyes raised as he heard quiet footsteps and saw Will Peters, the local police chief, sitting near them. "Our police chief is here, Devaney."

She shot a look at the older man, seeing for the first time Bradon sitting there. "Where did you come from?"

Bradon gave a quick grin. "That's my dog, Kade, who seems to think you need comfort. I can leave if you want."

Will shook his head at Bradon. "Devaney? May I call you that?" At her nod, he continued. "I am Will Peters. I want to help you solve this and get you back to the person you were and can be."

She finally nodded, her eyes going back to Blair. "I guess. I want this over." She stared down at the ring on her finger. "I need this over for Blair, so he can go on with his life."

Chapter 16

Gathering her thoughts and her courage, Devaney kept her eyes on Blair, a frown in place before she spoke.

"Blair, what do you do?"

"What do you mean? What do I do?"

"For a living. I know you were training as a mechanic but I don't know what you do."

"I am a mechanic, Devaney. Let me explain about the Barnabas Foundation. This building is the headquarters. We all have apartments here, as well as offices. We are paid by the Foundation but employed by local firms. That lets them hire more staff as they need to without having to worry about finances. We also volunteer in the community. I work with a local soccer club. Does that help?"

"It does but what is the Barnabas Foundation? I didn't hear about you're going to work for them before this all happened."

"It came up just as you left. The Barnabas Foundation was started by our employer and friend's father, who named it after his son, Barnabas, but also took it from the Barnabas in the Bible, to be encouragers to everyone we work with or meet."

She sighed. "Then I did hear right."

"What did you hear?" Will's question had her head flying around to look at him.

"That Blair was working for a charity of some kind. But I know that's not what this is."

"It is. Devaney, it is." Blair's voice held a tone she had not heard from him. "We are a charity. Just not like what you would think of one. Why would you say that?"

She shrugged. "I don't know. Just something I heard somewhere and I can't remember who." Her face paled. "It was him. He was behind me in a book store where I had taken shelter from a rainstorm. He talked about you and the Foundation, told me you were working for a company that was a coverup for illegal activities. I believed him. Blair, what did I do?"

He reached once more for her hand, his strong and tight on hers. "Tell us. Talk to us. Give us the details you can. Names if possible."

She nodded, a look of relief crossing her face. "I have carried this for so long." She struggled to continue. "But I know he's still out there. He threatened to kill Blair. Why I don't know."

"Talk to us, please, Devaney. Then we can sort it out. Will is going to take notes. So will Bradon. We'll get it figured out for you." Blair tightened his grasp on her hand, seeking to reassure her, even as Kade whined.

She searched the men's face and then nodded. "I will. I just don't know who he is or how he is connected to either one of us. I don't know that I have ever heard a name for him, although I have met people on the streets who know him and are terrified."

Shudders ran through her body. She wasn't quite sure where to start or even if the men would believe her. What she had gone through sounded like a bad movie or television series plot or a suspense novel that shouldn't have been written.

Chapter 17

Her mind wandered back in time, to the last few days of college. She and Blair had been planning their wedding, knowing they were in love and wanted to spend the rest of their lives with one another. She had remembered hearing Blair vaguely speak of a job offer he was considering in another province, but she hadn't sat down with him as he had asked. That wasn't something she was worried about. It didn't matter where they lived, she thought.

She had moved through the days leading up to their graduation in a fog, she thought. She didn't know the man who had approached her, had not wanted to talk to him, but he had forced her too. She had run from him, not feeling safe.

Devaney found the envelope taped to her apartment door the next morning, not moving at first to take it down. She finally did, opening it and pulling out the folded paper. She had frowned as she read it, not understanding what the man was asking for. Blair, she knew, didn't have anything that this man wanted. What was it he was asking for?

The threats against Blair had intensified. Devaney grew afraid for him, but couldn't talk to him. That was something she just didn't know how to do, and they talked about everything. She knew he was wanted to talk to her about the job he was taking, how it would move them from their home province. She had walked away at one point, leaving him staring after her.

Graduation day had arrived and she knew that at some point she had to talk to him. They had planned their wedding for a few days after that, then planned on moving across the country. She just couldn't do it. She had been threatened and so had Blair. Devaney had no idea what the man was asking for.

Blair had stared at her the day after graduation, not sure if he had heard her right.

"Devaney, talk to me. What are you saying?"

"Just that I need a day or so. I have something I need to do." She watched his face, seeing his disturbance on it, knowing he just didn't understand.

She had run from him, leaving him standing, staring after her before he ran to catch up with her, a hand on her arm stopping her.

Devaney had stood, hearing his pleas for her to talk to him, feeling the eyes watching her, the evil around them. She had finally shaken off his hand and ran, disappearing in the crowd. Blair had run after her, not finding her, standing with a hand on his head, looking. He had haunted her apartment over the next few days, seeking to find her wherever he was.

Blair had finally had to pack and move east, Devaney standing in the shadows watching, sorrow in her heart, her eyes rising to see a shadowy form standing across from her.

She had searched their hometown, looking for what it was, before she had moved to another town. That town became another town, another city, another province as she moved slowly across the country, not at peace, feeling herself tracking Blair, knowing that the man was following her or had someone following her.

Devaney had finally arrived in Ontario, tracking Blair as best she could. She knew he had been offered work with The Barnabas Foundation and had researched it in the public libraries of the towns she had lived in. She had been homeless, on the streets, staying in shelters, finding a cheap apartment as she could.

She stood one day, watching as he walked away from a store, a man with him that she thought must be a friend. She didn't see the man watching her. Devaney had turned that day, knowing Blair was safe, but she was no closer to what she was to find. That disturbed her. How could she keep him safe if she had no idea what that monster as she termed him was looking for?

Devaney had looked up about a week later, seeing the men approaching her, knowing he had found her. She ran for her car, a cheap little second hand car, all she could afford, and sped away from town, knowing the men were after her. She drove in a wild circle, knowing they were following her. She finally turned down a road, the road sliding away from her as she hit the ditch. She shoved open her door, her eyes wild as she searched, hearing a vehicle approaching. She ran for the side of the road and for the trees she could see, hearing the car stop and that voice once more. She made herself run faster, not caring that she was getting wet with the rain that was turning to sleet.

Devaney's feet slid out from under her and she tumbled to the ground, hitting hard and laying still.

I'll just rest a moment, she thought, and then get up.
They won't find me. I won't let them.

She didn't hear the other vehicles stopping or
see the emergency lights. She didn't feel the hands
reaching for her, turning her over, or tending to her.
She didn't feel the men lifting her to a stretcher or the
stretcher carried to the waiting ambulance.

Blair had stood, his eyes on her, walking
forward to touch her. She didn't know he was there
or she would have tried to flee once more. She didn't
hear his words that claimed her.

Devaney came back to the present, her eyes on
Blair, seeing the distress her words had caused.

"Devaney?" His voice reached out to her.

"I'm sorry, Blair. I can't do this." She was on
her feet, running from the room, Blair reaching for his
crutches before Brandon stopped him.

"Let me to, Blair. Let me talk to her." Brandon
followed her, catching up their jackets as he did so.

Chapter 18

Brandon watched Devaney closely as she paced the lobby of the building, not sure if she was heading for the outdoors or not. He approached her, laying a hand on her arm, causing her to jump.

"Brandon, isn't it?" At his nod, she sighed. "Blair sent you, didn't he?"

"No, I volunteered. He was going to come, but I think you need to talk to someone other than him." He nodded towards the seats, reaching for the bottles of water the security agent handed him. "Let's sit, okay?"

She moved to one of the couches, slumping down on it, her eyes on the bottle of water he had extended to her before she took it, rolling in her hands. Her eyes were on him.

"So, you wanted to talk?"

He grinned at her. "Not really. I think you just needed a friend to sit with you."

Devaney just shook her heard. "This is too hard, Brandon. I can't be near him."

"And he doesn't want you away from him. You're torn. You want to stay with him but you don't want to be there in case he gets hurt again."

"That sums part of it up." She leaned forward, setting the bottle of water on the table. "I don't know his name. I have gotten rid of everything he has left me over the years. The letters, the packages, the photos. I just couldn't handle it. I couldn't keep it."

"We understand, Devaney." Brandon wasn't sure where to head with his comments. "You did what you had to survive. You're not the same person you were back then."

"No, I'm not. And I'm not sure Blair will understand." She had not seen Blair moving up behind her, pausing at her words. "And I don't know how to keep him safe."

Blair sat, his arm sliding around Devaney, causing her to jump, and her face to whiten. He sighed. This is not going good, Lord. How do I reach her?

Devaney turned to him, shaking her head, and then rising, walking away from him. I can't do this, Lord. I need to find somewhere away from here.

Blair watched her walk away, not liking it, but knowing he had to. Brandon watched him closely.

"Blair?"

"She never told me. She just wouldn't talk about it. I couldn't help her. I tried to find her but she was hidden. No one would tell me where she was." He rested his hand on his leg for a moment before reaching for his crutches. "She'll run, Brandon, just to keep me safe. I can't let her do that."

"And how do you stop her?"

"I have no idea." Blair thumped away on his crutches, not seeing Devaney watching him, a worried look on her face.

—

83

She approached Blair, finally, waiting until he had turned to her.

"Blair, you have to stay away from me."

"It doesn't work that way, Devaney. Not any more. You can be sure he knows you're here. Why do you think we were run down in the parking lot? That was him, wasn't it?" Blair had to tamp down his anger, praying for release from it.

She nodded. "I know it was. That was one thing he had threatened to do." She sighed, her arms wrapping around herself. "I need to get out in the air, to walk outside."

Blair nodded, squinting at the darkening sky. "Tomorrow, love. I'll get you out for a walk tomorrow."

Chapter 19

Blair watched Devaney closely the next morning as she stood outside the building, her jacket open. He could tell she was enjoying being outside. He moved towards her, his crutches thumping as he did so, causing her to turn.

"Blair? Are you sure about this?"

He shrugged. "About as sure as I am about anything lately." He nodded towards a path. "We can take that one if you like. It's not too long a path, leads to a little sitting area."

"Oh, really? You didn't tell me that."

Blair grinned. "Barnabas has set up lots of little areas like that. He was planning ahead, knowing at some point we would need them. He has a playground in the works now that Baird and Benen are married. And the ice rink down near the road. He'll let the town use it at times, but it's for us."

Devaney thought through what he was saying, even as she walked beside him.

"You like working here?"

"I don't work here on site, Devaney. I work off site for a garage. And I volunteer as well with the youth group at church, besides holding courses for ladies to learn about their cars."

"You do that? You never liked to teach."

He shrugged. "It's come with the territory. I've changed, Devaney. I'm not quite the man you fell in love with."

"We all do." Devaney stopped at the end of the walk, her arms wrapping around herself. "Blair, we need to go back. Something's wrong." Her scream was cut off by the hand around her mouth, even as she saw the men approaching Blair, shoving his crutches away from him, and dragging him to a van. She was shoved inside, not allowed to touch him, her eyes huge with her fright.

Hours later, Brandon and Breck appeared at the sitting area, Brandon reaching for the crutches, both men searching for the tow, unable to find them.

"Brandon?"

"This is what Devaney feared. She didn't want to stay around Blair. That's what she told me. She was afraid he would be taken." He sighed. "Now we have to call in Will, don't we?"

Breck nodded, pointing back towards the building. "I know we do. Barnabas had a premonition of this, did you know?"

"No, I didn't but it's par for the course. This is what always happens, isn't it?"

They searched over the next few days, not finding their friends, not sure where they were. Three days after the two disappeared, an envelope appeared on the seat of the bench. Benen reached for it, searching the area, before he left on a run, heading for Barnabas.

"I found this, Barnabas. On the bench in that area." Benen breathed heavily, trying to regain his breath.

"You did?" Barnabas stared at it, seeing it addressed to himself. "This is strange, you know. Addressed to me."

"I know. Are you opening it?"

"I guess I have to, don't I?" He pulled out the flap and then the letter, seeing objects drop to the desk top. "What are these?"

"Barnabas, that's the pin from his college. He always wears it. I don't know why though, he's never said. And that's a ring I saw on Devaney." Benen was more worried than he let on.

"So they are." Barnabas unfolded the letter, a frown in place. "This doesn't say much, other than they have them. No ransom demands. No information as to when they'll be in touch."

"So, now what? You have to go to Will, don't you?"

"I should, but not today. There was no evidence there, was there?"

"No, other than that. No footprints, if that's what you're asking."

Barnabas nodded. "Let's meet this afternoon, after everyone's back. Bring all the research I know you have all be doing. We'll see where we stand then."

Benen nodded, knowing there was little they could do, except wait. The letter, he felt was bizarre to say the least.

Chapter 20

The men milled around the conference room early that evening, concern for Blair uppermost in their mind. They wanted to head out to find him, but didn't know exactly where to look. They all turned as Barnabas entered, a sheaf of papers in his hand, before he looked up and nodded, each man finding a seat.

"Break up in groups, please. Let's spend time in prayer first." Barnabas looked over at Doc, who had entered with him, and motioned him over. "Doc?"

"We need to pray, Barnabas. I feel their very lives are in danger."

Three hours later, the men rose, not having made much progress in their search for the missing two. Talking quietly among themselves, they walked away, Breck watching carefully for signs of extreme stress or worry. He turned back to Doc and Barnabas.

"Doc? You're not saying much."

"There's not much I can say, Breck. I am worried about them but without knowing where they are, we can't go in and find them. I think that's the whole purpose of that letter. To drive up our anxiety and not give away any information."

—

"I think you're right, and it's succeeding." Barnabas reached to gather his papers, following the two men to the door, and switching off the lights, ensuring the door was closed and locked behind him. "I just want them back."

"We all do." Doc paused for a moment. "Devaney has struck a chord with Anna. She wants to mother that lady and can't. Devaney just won't let her."

"It comes from being on her own for so many years and living on the streets. I'm not sure how to reach her, if we even can." Breck walked away, leaving the other two men exchanging glances.

Buckley ran for Barnabas the next day, his phone out as he did so. He slid to a halt in the office door, not seeing Barnabas. Amy, his secretary, looked up in surprise.

"He's not here, Buckley. He had a meeting out of town."

"That's right. I did forget that." Buckley spun and was gone, leaving Amy staring after him before she shook her head and immersed herself back into her work

Buckley stood in the lobby, searching for who, he wasn't sure. Bradon approached, his head tilted to watch his friend.

"Buckley? You look lost."

Spinning, Buckley stared at Bradon, then waved his phone. "I have word. Come with me. I think I know where they're at."

"You do? How?" Bradon's step matched Buckley as they headed for Buckley's car.

"A friend, you might say. He told someone at the mission, who sent me word. We need to move, before they disappear again."

"Should we not have help?"

Buckley shook his head. "Not until I know for sure they're where he says. I don't want to raise hope."

The two men stared at the ramshackle building on the outskirt of a neighbouring village before they exchanged glances.

"They're here?"

Buckley nodded. "You can see the tracks of vehicles in and out. There shouldn't be." He opened his door, carefully closing it so as not to make a sound. Bradon followed, their steps quiet as they moved towards the building.

"There. I can see Blair's footsteps heading in but not out."

"And those would be Devaney's. This is bizarre, you know."

"I know." Buckley looked around, not seeing anyone or feeling like they were being watched. "Let's do this."

Bradon nodded, his hand reaching of the broken-down door and pulling it open.

They searched, keeping as quiet as they could, before Bradon's hand stopped Buckley and then he pointed. They moved forward, hands reaching for

Blair and then Devaney, picking them up. They looked behind them as they drove away, a frown on both men's faces. It had been too easy, Bradon thought. Just too easy.

Chapter 21

Doc watched closely as Devaney's head twisted on the pillow. He had assessed her and then let Anna help her to their spare room she had been using. He frowned, his thoughts puzzles, before he turned and walked away, heading for the other room where Blair was ensconced. Blair had roused when they reached the building, his head shaking when questioned.

"I don't know who they were. I don't think they were the ones after Devaney and then after me. It doesn't make sense." He looked up at Breck who had appeared in the kitchen. "It just doesn't make sense. They didn't question us, just left us. I think that last day, was it only yesterday, they drugged either our food or water."

Doc nodded at that. "I suspect that's what they did. Let's get you to bed, Blair. We can talk in the morning."

Barnabas had stood, his eyes watchful, as he listened. He sighed. He had spoken to Will earlier, letting him know they had the two, but he wanted it kept very quiet. Agreeing, Will had sent an officer out to search the building, who had found the two men searching for the missing couple and arrested them.

Breck turned to Barnabas. "What is going on? This does not make sense."

"No, it doesn't. I think Blair is right. There are two different parties at work here. Find the men. I think the chapel is the right place to meet."

Breck stared at him for a moment, and then nodded. "We need to talk to them. When's Will heading this way?"

"He's not, not tonight. He wants to see what they find in that building. I don't suspect they'll find much."

Breck shook his head. "I doubt it. Buckley seemed to think they were just dumped there." He looked around as he heard a noise, a frown appearing on his face. "Devaney?"

Devaney halted her steps, her eyes huge with fright. "Who are you? Where am I?"

"It's Breck and Barnabas, Devaney."

It took her a moment to understand and then she nodded, moving past them to open the fridge, reaching for a bottle of juice and then into the cupboard for a glass before she turned to stare at them.

"Where's Blair?"

"He's sleeping, Devaney." Breck pulled out a chair, motioning for her to sit. "Can you tell us what happened?"

She gave an unladylike snort, causing smiles to break out on the men's faces. "What happened? I went for a walk, Blair with me, and then someone's there. They took his crutches from him and then took us away." She sat back, lost in thought. "It's not the man after us. It was someone else. He told me he wanted that other man, and he would use us to bring him out.” She looked up, fear on her face. “Does that make sense?

“It does, Devaney. We will need to talk more. Can you describe this man?”

She shook her head. “No, I can’t, but I feel like I know him from out west. Does that even sound right?”

“It could. We’ll need a list of men around his age from out there, if you can/”

She nodded and then yawned, on her feet and moving away from them, leaving them to stare after her.

“Did she just do that?”

Barnabas laughed at Breck’s comment. “She did. She’s not used to being around friends and how to react or act anymore. She’ll get there.”

Chapter 22

A week later, Devaney was on a search. She needed something and only going to town would work. She sighed. This is not right, Lord. I need my freedom and don't have it. She spun in a circle, before heading for the door. A walk might help, she decided, heading for the road and town, not realizing how far a walk it would be. She sank onto a bench at the edge of town, her eyes watchful, feeling someone monitoring her. She shuddered. Lord, I want this over and it doesn't appear that it will be any time soon.

Burnie paused in his walk back to his car and looked around. Yes, that was Devaney, and she was on her own. He changed directions, to come to a stop in front of her before he sat beside her, not saying a word.

"What? You're not telling me I shouldn't have done this?" She peeked at him, not sure of him. She hadn't gotten to know all the men to know how they'd react.

Burnie shrugged. "It's a free country. If you want to leave, you can. We would rather you didn't. Blair can't handle you leaving again."

She sighed. "I know. I needed to come to town and couldn't find anyone to bring me. I don't have my car back yet. Blair said they were working on it for me."

Burnie's hand stopped in its movement of running along his jeans. "You walked?" At her nod, he stared at her. "Do you know how far that is?"

"I do now." She stared towards town. "I have to get some stuff, but I think I'm too tired to walk that far."

"What do you need?"

"I have to get some clothes and some shampoo and toothpaste. I can't keep using Anna's. And I don't have many clothes." She was almost in tears.

Burnie stood, a hand reached out for her. "Come on. Pretend I'm Blair for a bit. I'll walk you down to the nearest store and you can shop. Then we'll head back for home."

She stopped, her body still as she heard his words, before she spoke. "Is that what it is, Burnie? Home?"

"I think it is. You've been running for so many years, Devaney, that I don't think you understand how welcome you are there." He looked around, feeling someone near him, but not seeing anyone. "How be we head off, and then I'll take you back to Blair?"

"Right. Blair. He'll tell me off, I just know it."

Burnie laughed. "Not Blair. He'll just look at you with that question on his face."

She gave a small smile. "I don't know him anymore, Burnie. I just don't know him. And right now, I need to stay away from him."

"He's not going to let you, you do know that, don't you?" He grinned down at her as he held the store door open. "Go on, get what you need." He paused. "If it's money stopping you from getting what you want, don't let it. We can work it out."

She stared at him for a moment, not sure on his words, before she moved away, quickly finding what she wanted and then standing in line, searching for the man who had haunted her for so many years. He was near, she knew. She looked through the people waiting to pay, seeing Burnie watching her and then looking around.

"Did you get what you wanted?" His quiet question broke into her thoughts as he reached for the bags in her hand.

"I think so." She sighed. "I'm not sure anymore on anything, Burnie. I feel that God has abandoned me. I don't trust that He's there with me. I used to know He was."

"He is, Devaney. He has never ever left you." He sighed to himself as he closed the car door, watching as she twisted to stare around her. Lord, why me? How do I get through to her?"

Blair stopped near Burnie's car, a question on his face, as Burnie slid from it before heading for the trunk. He watched as Devaney took the bags she was handed, a quick glance at him, before she walked away, heading for Anna and Doc's apartment.

"Burnie?"

Burnie turned at the question in Blair's voice, not quite sure how to respond. He gathered his thoughts, hearing the chirping of the birds in the shrubs near the building.

"She walked to town, Blair."

"She did what?" Blair spun to stare after Devaney.

"She walked to town. She had to get some things, she said, and didn't know any other way to get there." He looked down, then back up, distress on his face. "Blair, she didn't ask for help. She just walked all that way on her own."

"And she could have disappeared, and we would never have known." Blair's eyes slid shut, before he turned back to Burnie. "How do we do this, Burnie?"

Burnie shrugged, a slight smile on his face. "That's something you'll have to figure out, Blair. We can't do that for you." He nodded towards the building. "She's been on her own for too long. She doesn't realize others will help her. And she says God isn't there anymore, that He's abandoned her." Burnie walked away, leaving Blair to stare after him, before his head slid back and his eyes closed.

God, please, help my lady. She needs to feel that touch from You, that healing from touching the garment. How do we do this?

Chapter 23

Anna turned from the door the next day, her voice welcoming both Berneen and Cadee as they entered, heading for her kitchen.

"What can I get for you ladies?"

"Whatever you're having, Anna. You know us. We're not fancy." Berneen stood for a moment, watching as Devaney slumped on the couch. "Devaney?"

Devaney jumped, not having heard the ladies enter, her eyes huge.

Berneen slipped to a sitting position on the couch, her hand out to touch Devaney's. "I'm sorry. I didn't mean to frighten you."

"That's okay. I jump at everything. I have for years." She looked up as Anna handed her a mug. "You're here to visit Anna." She made a move to stand before Berneen's hand tightened on hers.

"We're here to visit Anna, yes. But we are here to visit you as well." Berneen exchanged a glance with Cadee, who nodded. "We haven't gotten to know you, but we would like to. You've seen us around. I'm Baird's Berneen, and that's Benen's Cadee. And we both have a story of an adventure to share with you. God spoke to both of us this morning, telling us we needed to come see you today."

Devaney stared at the two younger women before she turned to Anna, who was nodding.

"That's true, Devaney. They've come to my place, but you're the one they're here to see. They asked if you would be here today. It's up to you if you stay and visit with us. That is your choice. We really would like you to stay." Anna waited, a prayer in her heart that Devaney would do just that.

Devaney studied her and then turned to Berneen, searching her face before she did the same with Cadee. She finally shrugged, setting her mug on the coaster on the black walnut end table, and tucking the blanket she had over her closer around her. She wanted to visit with these ladies. Devaney had not had an opportunity to do that since college, she thought. I need this. I can do this, can't I?

Berneen had been watching her face closely and saw when she decided to stay. She breathed a sigh of relief. God had impressed on her heart that morning that Devaney needed a friend, someone just to stand beside her.

"So, Anna, what verses do you have this morning?" Cadee smiled at Devaney as she looked startled. "Anna always has a verse for us, Devaney. Today, I sense that it's one for you."

Anna just shook her head. "Not yet, dear. I'm still working through that."

Berneen nodded. "That you do, Anna. You don't know how many times I have needed those verses." She turned to Devaney. "Did Blair tell you about our adventure?"

Devaney shook her head. "We haven't talked. It's not likely that he will." She frowned at the looks on the faces. "What kind of adventure would you have had? You're married, settled here."

Berneen and Cadee began to laugh, causing the other younger woman to stare at them and then turn to Anna.

"They did have adventures, my dear. I don't know how they survived them." Anna rose, heading for the kitchen, returned with a tray with a large teapot, cream, sugar and a plate of sandwiches and squares on it. "We'll need this, I think." She looked at Berneen. "You were the first, Berneen. You can start."

Berneen nodded, a momentary look of pain crossing her face. "It wasn't fun, Devaney. I had been kidnapped, held for month, and then Baird was kidnapped. The guys came in and found him, he insisted I had to come. We were kidnapped again the very next day, along with Buckley. He was beaten to the point of almost dying. The only way to stop that was for me to marry him. I did. Do you know how hard that was? Anyway, despite what they threw at us, and despite me having to raise my teenaged brother, Darby, we fell in love somewhere in there." She looked up, seeing the shock on Devaney's face. "It was brutal, I must admit. God was there."

Cadee nodded. "I know he was with us, Devaney. Benen and I were old friends, losing touch. My parents were missionaries in South America. Dad had written to Benen to come visit and he did. I didn't know at the time that someone wanted me dead and the only way for me to get out of the country was a name change. Dad asked Benen to marry me, to provide that name change. Like Baird and Berneen, we had a lot of difficulty, almost losing one another at some point. But Benen is the love of my life. He always was. God was there for us as well. That I have no doubt of."

Devaney stared at the two women, her eyes huge, her mouth opening and closing. "There is no way you two went through that."

The three women with her laughed.

"But they did, Devaney." Anna's hand reached to lay on Devaney's head. "They did. All our guys became involved at some point or another, including Doc. When Berneen got here, she was very determined she had to leave. She needed to find her brother, who she had put into hiding. Once we had him here with her, she settled down. Well, sort of."

Berneen and Cadee laughed at Anna's phrasing.

"I did, Devaney." She shared a look with Cadee. "I know how Blair feels about you. If he hasn't said, he is still deeply in love with you. He wants the best for you. If it means letting you go, he will. He won't trap you into staying."

Devaney's eyes dropped to her hands, hands she had twisted into the blanket.

"I can't stay. I'm too dangerous for him to know." She blinked rapidly against the gathering tears.

Anna gave a small sound and then had Devaney wrapped in her arms, holding her as she finally wept. Wept for lost opportunities, for the danger she had been in, for the years she had lost. She wept for the danger she felt she had brought to Blair.

Anna looked up as she heard footsteps and saw Blair hesitating in the doorway before he was over to Devaney, taking Anna's spot, his beloved wrapped in his arms as she wept. His own tears wet her hair, as Anna and the other two ladies moved away, heading for the kitchen. Doc took one look at Anna and swept her into a hug.

"Whatever you said, you three, got through to her, I think." Doc watched the couple in the living room. "Thank you, ladies. Now, maybe we can figure out how to keep those two safe."

"We need to, Doc. We need to. I sense a growing cloud of danger overhanging them." Berneen reached to hug the older couple as did Cadee, before they walked away, the door closing softly behind them.

Chapter 24

Blair stood later that night, staring out the living room window of his apartment, a hand resting on the glass, his eyes on the stars in the dark blue sky. His thoughts were muddled. How do I help her, Lord? How do I do this? How do I reach through to the lady I know and love?

He turned as he heard a tap at his door and frowned. It was late, he thought, for someone to be there. He walked through to open the door, not seeing anyone there. He stepped out, the boot case on his foot tapping loud on the tile floor and looked around. He shrugged, turning back to his door, frowning as he saw the envelope taped to it. Sighing, Blair reached for it, not recognizing the handwriting.

Dropping the envelope on his desk, he stared at it, not sure if he wanted to open it. He felt fear for a moment, not for himself as much as for Devaney. He finally reached to untuck the flap, pulling out the card in it.

Blair reached for a pen, using it to open the card. A sympathy card, he thought. This is bizarre. He read the threat printed inside, a threat against his lady. He had no idea what they wanted from him. He had nothing. Blair raised his head, his thoughts drifting back in years, to coming home from school as a young child, and not finding anyone home. He felt once more the fear he had felt that day, the anxiety, the stress. He had been thankful for his foster parents, but had longed for someone of his own. Was his mother somehow involved in this?

Rising early the next morning, Blair sought out Barnabas, handing him the card without a word. Barnabas read it, his eyes rising Blair.

"What do you make of this? And someone once more got in to the building."

"I have no idea, Barnabas. All I know is that my lady is threatened, and I don't like it."

"I didn't think you did. Are you off to work this morning?"

Blair nodded. "I am. There are some things I can do, now that I'm not on crutches." He paused, a grimace on his face. "How do I leave her? I need to talk to her but she won't talk to me."

"Let me. Maybe I can get through to her. Will was heading this way later this morning." Barnabas studied Blair, reaching to lay a hand on his shoulder. "Let me pray for you two. I sense this is getting worse for you."

"It is. And no matter what anyone thinks, we are not a couple. Not anymore. I suspect she'll hand me back her ring and then disappear again." Blair finally moved away, to where Bradon waited to drive him to the garage.

Devaney stood, shock on her face, as she had heard the words Blair had uttered. Did he really think that? She stood, sorrow on her face, not seeing Branigan watching her. Barnabas and Branigan shared a look before Branigan moved towards her.

"Devaney?"

She jumped as she heard someone speak beside her and glared at Branigan. "What is it with you guys? Do you always sneak up on someone?"

Branigan laughed but the mirth didn't reach his eyes. "Not always, but I would say you were deep in thought." He reached to tuck her arm into his. "Come with me, to my office. We need to have a talk."

"That's all you guys want to do, is talk. I want to find this guy, whoever it is"

"And we will." Branigan unlocked his office, switching on the light and pointing to a chair, watching as Devaney sat before he sat in a chair beside her, watching her eyes skitter around the room, a frown still on her face.

"Branigan? What?" She stared at him, a puzzled look on her face.

Branigan shook his head. "Nothing. Now, about what you overheard?"

"I heard. He's being threatened."

"Not him, Devaney. Not this time." He watched with compassion as she continued to stare at him, a puzzled look on her face before her eyes closed.

"It's me, isn't it?" She refused to look up. "I need to leave."

"If you leave, so will Blair. He was follow you, wherever you go. And that means he'll be hurt or killed, just to wreak revenge for something." Branigan paused, praying for the right words. "He still loves you deeply, Devaney. I am not sure that he would even stay if you left."

She nodded. "I think you are right. But how do we find this monster? I have talked to the police before. In different cities and towns. Blair doesn't know that that monster had me physically assaulted and beaten. I have a laceration on my shoulder that has just healed." She looked up at Branigan. "I want this over. I don't want to live like this anymore."

Her arms wrapped around herself, Devaney stood and began to pace, Branigan's eyes on her, a hand reaching for a pad of paper and a pen. She spun, staring at him, before she sat back down, her mouth opening and closing.

"What do you do, Branigan?"

"What do you mean?"

"Your occupation. Do you have an investigator on staff?"

He shook his head. "No, we don't. But I know of someone I can contact. As to me? I am a security systems specialist. I install or review security systems." His head tilted as she sighed and her eyes slid closed. "Devaney?"

"Then, you all do something different? Is that what you're saying?"

"We do. All of us have our own career or work. We also volunteer in our spare time."

"Do you have to volunteer?"

"No, it's not part of our contract, but it's part of who we are as one of the Barnabas Foundation people. The concept for the Foundation is to provide encouragement, and you can guess that comes in many ways. For me, I also teach self defence to teens.”

“Okay. Then, where do we start?” She pointed to his pen. “You plan on writing this down?”

“That I do, Devaney. And with your permission, I will pass it on to all of us. That way, each of us will search and then combine our resources. We also have friends we can pull in, if we need to.”

She nodded. “Okay. So. Where do I begin?”

Chapter 25

Her mind racing as she thought through the events in her past, Devaney leaned back in her chair, her hands rubbing against one another. Where do I start? Lord, this is so hard, but You've said You are with me. That if I seek You, I will find You. That's what I want, Lord. To find You once more.

Branigan waited, his eyes watchful, turning as he heard the door open, and Blair enter. He frowned. Blair was to be at work today.

Blair's head shook in the negative as he seated himself behind Devaney before his eyes sought her, a frown on his face. What was she up to now, he wondered? Barnabas had called him back from work, just stating he needed to be there, that Devaney needed him.

"Devaney?" Branigan's gentle voice broke into her thoughts, and she jumped.

"Branigan! I forgot you were here."

"I know you did. Now, can you give names, towns, events. I know we've done this, but this time I want you to really concentrate. Give me anything that comes to mind." He pointed his pen at her, a smile lighting his face. "It doesn't matter how minor or insignificant it is." He paused. "Blair's here."

"He is?" She spun, her eyes huge as she looked at him, despair on her face, but also the acknowledgement that he did need to be there. She waited as he drew his chair up beside her.

"Barnabas told me I needed to be here. Do I? I can leave if you'd rather."

She shook her head. "No, I think you should be here. I think, anyway." She blew out a breath, her eyes scrunching closed, as she tried to control her emotions.

He watched, before he reached to hug her, and then prayed for her. She relaxed in his arms, feeling that she had come home, that God really was with her.

Branigan waited when Blair finished, his eyes on Devaney, as she rubbed at her face before she looked at him.

"Okay, so, we should start."

"That would be good. How about you tell me what it was like when you were little? I know you were in foster care."

"I was. I don't remember being anywhere else, I don't think. I was shifted from home to home, I have no idea why. That made for a difficult childhood. I always felt the one left out, the fifth wheel, the unwanted one. That was until the last foster home. They made me feel like I was part of their family. I know they wanted to adopt me. They told me that. But they didn't, and I don't know why." She searched Blair's face to see if he had an answer for that, but he just shook his head. "That's where Blair and I met. I mean, it wasn't easy being a foster kid. It never is. Anyway, we made it through college. I studied business courses, but that really wasn't what I wanted to do. I'm not sure now why I did.

"But that last month or so, I could feel someone watching me. He finally started appearing behind him, leaving messages on my phone. I have no idea how he got that number. I would have letters in my box that were hand delivered. Photos. He threatened Blair, telling me Blair had something he wanted or needed him to do. He kept changing what he was saying. And no, I didn't keep any of them. I threw them away. I was so scared. When Blair asked me what was up, I couldn't tell him. I had to walk away. I wanted to find this man and stop the madness."

She paused, reaching for the bottle of water Blair handed her, sipping it, thoughts racing through her mind, before she capped the bottle again, rolling it in her hands.

Devaney finally started to speak again, her voice low and halting.

"He chased me across the country, from province to province, city to city. Here, Branigan, let me have your paper." She took it and began to write, turning over page after page before she sat back, drained, handing it back to Branigan. "This should help. I have listed everything I can think of." She turned as Blair reached for her, her face buried against him, a shuddering sigh drawn from her.

Branigan watched her for a moment, his eyes raising to Blair, watching him closely before he shook his head and his eyes dropped to the paper. Reading through it, he drew in a deep breath, realizing just how vicious the man after Devaney had been, and just how close she had been to devastation or death. They needed to find him, and find him soon.

They spoke for a while longer, before Blair, his arm around her, led Devaney away, desperate to find a place where she would be safe. It didn't seem that she was safe here, not any better that Berneen and Cadee had been. Lord, now what? Where do we go from here?

Chapter 26

Blair paced the walkways around the building, his cast thumping each time it hit the concrete, his mind on Devaney. How do we do this, Lord? I am at a loss. We need to find this person, and stop him. Devaney won't survive unless we do, or she'll run and I'll never find her again.

He turned as he felt someone near him, his mouth open to yell, before he snapped it closed, his hands going up into the air. Blair walked towards the man and then past him as the weapon held on him didn't waver. He knew he had to get away, but didn't see an opening to do just that. With his leg in a cast, he couldn't run, but he didn't think he could outrun a bullet. He walked towards the path that led deep into the forest, his eyes in constant movement to try and find a way to escape.

Slumping back against the truck seat, Blair's eyes held steady on the man beside him, the weapon still in evidence, even as he felt the truck move away from the building, away from safety. He had no idea who these men were, or what they wanted, just that they seemed to want him. He was pulled from the vehicle when it finally stopped in the town, pushed towards a factory building, and then up narrow metal stairs. The door opened and he was once more shoved forward, staggering to keep his feet, before he spun, hands up to defend himself. Blair frowned, his eyes on the man standing watching him.

The man pointed to a chair and Blair was shoved down into it, the man behind him holstering his weapon and then standing at the door. Blair waited, not sure what was going on, his eyes steady on the man walking towards him.

"Blair? This is not what you think. I wanted to speak with you but you just don't seem to be on your own."

"No, Timothy. I'm not. This is why." Blair stared at Timothy Meadows, a friend, he thought. "What do you want? Could you not have just picked up the phone? It would have been a lot simply. This time, you're be arrested for kidnapping."

Timothy sighed. "I know, Blair, I know. I just have to talk to you. Now that you're here, I'm not sure how to proceed."

"Just start talking, Timothy, or I'm leaving. Your men won't stop me." Blair felt anger rising in him and worked to tamp it down.

Timothy paced before he stopped in front of Blair. "I know your lady is in town. We've seen her around for a good month or more. She hasn't said anything but we've seen her watching you. You didn't know this, I gather. We have also seen men watching her, as well as a woman. Who they are, we're working on." He looked up at the man standing at the door, nodding. The man handed Blair a folder. "In this, Blair, are all the details we could find, as well as photos of them. I would take this to Will, but then I'd have to explain what I do on the side, and that I don't want to."

"And just what do you do on the side, Timothy? Tell me that."

Timothy sighed, his eyes raising to the ceiling as if seeking direction before he looked back at Blair. "I don't want to break a confidence but this is what I do. I am an agent for an organization that tracks people who are involved in national crimes. The ones after you are just such people. I know you are an orphan, Blair, that your father died and that your mother disappeared. We have looked into it." He paused once more, compassion on his face. "We have found her grave. I'm sorry."

Blair's hand rested heavily on the folder. "There is proof in here?" At Timothy's nod, he bowed his head, working to control his emotions. "But I don't understand how whoever it is, this monster as Devaney calls him, wants me. I have nothing that he would want. In fact, I have nothing other than what I have gathered over the last few years."

"That's what I thought." Timothy leaned towards him, tapping the paperwork. "Go through that. Have your friends go through it. I just ask that you don't give it to Will, not just yet. There is still something missing, and we're working on that for you." He looked up at the man near the door and nodded before he turned and walked away.

Blair sat, his eyes on Timothy, who he knew from church. How did this all come into play he wondered? He stood at the touch on his shoulder, finding the man who had been at the door standing there, an apologetic look on his face.

“We apologize, Blair. We weren’t sure if you would have come with us.”

“I would have, if you had asked, and told me why. Weapons weren’t necessary. Now, take me home. Next time, if there is a next time, just ask.”

Chapter 27

Hands to her mouth, Devaney stared at Blair, not sure that she had heard him correctly. She thought she had heard him say that he had been taken away at gunpoint, to meet someone he knew from church, who handed him the folder he now had in his hands, and then just let him walk away.

"That doesn't happen, Blair."

Blair gave a tired smile. He was sore, the leg was hurting from being on his feet, and now his lady doubted his word.

"It really happened, Devaney." His voice was weary and he turned from her to sit, seeing all of his friends standing there, Berneen and Cadee flanking Devaney. He shook his head as he motioned to Barnabas. "Here, take this. Timothy said he's been doing some research. He's included photos of the men and woman watching Devaney." He drew a shuddering breath, his eyes sliding closed. "He also said he found my Mom's grave."

Devaney was seated beside him, her arms around him, before he had finished, tears sparkling on her face. She knew how much he had hoped his mother was still alive, that she would be back in his life.

"Did they say how?" Breck's voice broke through the stunned silence.

Blair shrugged. "I haven't read it yet. I just got back." He leaned forward, elbows on his knees, his face buried in his hands. "I don't know how that relates to this, but it must. In some way it must or Timothy would not have included it."

He looked up as he heard footsteps. "And there's Will. I can't talk to him right now." He was on his feet, disappearing up the stairs, Devaney beside him.

Will watched him walk away and sighed. Another one running from me, Lord? Why don't they just talk to me?

"Barnabas? When did he get back?"

Barnabas shrugged, his eyes moving to each man and then the two ladies. "About an hour ago, I think. We were gathering to go looking for him and he walked in. He hasn't said much."

"Is he going to talk to me at all?" Will heard the footsteps of the men and two ladies as they walked away, leaving Barnabas standing alone with him.

"I don't know, Will. I honestly don't know. I hope he does. I pray that, but right now, he's hurting and so is Devaney."

Will nodded. "I do need to speak with her at some point over the next couple of days. I've been working on some of those names. They're nasty people, to put it milder. She's in far graver danger than she realizes."

"She knows, Will. She knows. She's not in denial. Devaney is trying to come up with a way to lead them away from Blair, but keep herself safe at the same time." Barnabas' hand rubbed against the folder. "Right now, I don't think she'll take off. But if she does, Blair will either go with her or track her down. And that worries me."

"It does me, too." Will squinted at his watch. "Tell them to call me tomorrow. I'm off but I'll be around home. Use my cell number." He looked back up, his eyes on his young friend. "Don't let them leave, Barnabas. No matter what you have to do. Keep them here."

"We'll do our best, but they are free agents, Will. We can't stop them if they want to walk away."

"Blair won't. He's too happy here." Will shook his head. "Let me rephrase that. He's happy here but he's not sure if Devaney will be. It hinges on her."

Barnabas nodded. "Berneen and Cadee spent time with her the other day. She was stunned to hear of their stories, and how they married the way they did. Anna said she was really thoughtful afterwards, and more softened towards them and she thought more softened towards God."

"That's our prayer, Barnabas. That she softens towards God. Once she's done that, she'll be more open to Blair."

Barnabas shook his head. "I don't see that. She's watching Blair to see how he's reacting to her. I can see her reaching out to him in a way she didn't when she was first here. She's worried he'll be hurt worse than he has been."

"That's true." Will pulled out his phone as he felt it vibrate, scanning the test. "We've got one of the men, Barnabas. He was just outside your property."

"I gathered they've been around there. Let's hope he talks. I want this over with."

Will nodded. "So do I. But what if this happens to everyone else? Have you given that a thought?"

Barnabas stared at him before he shook his head. "I pray it doesn't, but if it does, we'll go through it with God's help."

Chapter 28

Pacing her bedroom that night, Devaney's heart was broken for Blair. She knew how much he had looked for his mother, waiting for her to come back, when he was young. She didn't imagine it had changed as an adult.

Devaney turned to watch the door, then watched the clock, sighing as she saw it was only five in the morning. She walked quietly to the kitchen, making a cup of tea, and then settling down on the couch, a blanket over her, her hand reaching for Anna's Bible. She idly turned the pages, stopping to read the verses Anna had underlined and the comments she had made. Her eyes stopped on one and she read and re-read it.

Is this still true, Lord? Will You be found of me? I used to think that but then life got in the way. I want that back, Lord, the sense that You are with me. Tears flowed down into her heart, her face dry, as she waited, listened and prayed.

Doc paused as he saw her before he headed for the kitchen himself. Making himself a coffee and reaching for a fresh cup of tea for Devaney, he sat in his favourite chair, a smile on his face as she looked up with a word of thanks.

"No thanks are necessary." He nodded towards the Bible. "Anna's?"

"It is. It is like reading her life story to go through it."

"That is it. She was told by her parents to never mark a Bible, but she said she had to. It was a love letter from her Father and her best friend. She had to respond."

Devaney's face grew more thoughtful. "That's how it should be, isn't it? I've missed that. I don't even have a Bible now. I lost it somewhere and just never had enough money to replace it. Or I guess, enough to replace something I didn't think was necessary any longer." She looked up at him, devastation on her face. "What did I do, Doc?"

"You didn't do anything. At some point, we all fail and fall. Just read David's psalms. The Good Lord is always with you, whether you feel Him or not. He has promised never to leave you or forsake you." He watched with compassion as her face crumpled, and she wept silently, finally sitting up and wiping at her face.

"Devaney, where do you go from here?" Doc waited, knowing he was asking something she might not be ready or willing to answer.

She shrugged. "I don't really know, Doc. We need to find the ones after Blair. I'm not sure where I stand with him or where I want to."

"He loves you deeply, Devaney. He has never dated, has shown no interest in any ladies here. There has been interest on their part, but he just moves through life, his focus on God and his work."

"That sounds like him." She frowned at Doc as her mind thought through what she had undergone over the years. "Doc, how do I figure out who it is?"

"What do you mean?"

"I need to figure out who it is. I think we know the person behind what's been going on. They seem to know things about us that strangers wouldn't."

Doc nodded slowly, before he rose, beckoning her to follow him.

"Sit. You do know how to use a computer word processing program?"

"I think I still do. I studied that at college." She stared at the screen. "A database, is what you're thinking."

"That's right. We list all the names you can think of. Their relationship to one another. Their relationship to either you or Blair. I'll leave you to get started. Anna's going to be up soon and she needs to be at a meeting by nine. I'm off to start breakfast. Call me if you need me."

Devaney shot him a quick glance as he walked away and then turned back to the computer, her fingers finding the keyboard. It was slow at first but then her fingers and mind began to work together. Lord, is this You? Are You doing this? Help me to do this right, so that we can solve whatever it is and find whoever it is.

She finally sat back, her eyes on her work, before she rose, heading for the kitchen. She stretched, stiff from sitting so long. Doc eyed her as she entered the kitchen before he reached for her cup of tea and pointed to the table for her to sit.

"You've not taken a break, Devaney."

She sighed, rubbing at her neck and shoulders. "No, I didn't. I used to get lost when I was doing this kind of stuff." She looked up at him. "I need to talk to someone."

"Who?"

"I need to talk to someone who does IT. I need some advice."

Doc began to laugh. "Benen and Cadee will be here shortly. In fact, Cadee and Anna are planning a meal for us. Benen is in IT."

"Oh, wonderful. Where is he?" She went to rise, surprised to find hands on her shoulders stopping her from rising.

"He'll be here shortly. He just had to stop at their apartment." Blair slid into a seat beside her. "What have you been up to today?"

"Working on a database. I need you to look it over." Again, she went to rise, surprised to find Blair's hands holding hers and keeping her from rising. "Blair?"

"Doc says he found you all day in that chair, sitting crosslegged I would suspect for most of it?" Blair grinned at the look on her face. "I'll take a look at it. But you need a break. Anna and Doc have asked us to stay for a meal. I want that. Benen will be here and he will take a look at it for you. So will I. We'll solve this, Devaney. We will solve this."

Devaney looked around as she heard voices, seeing Anna, Benen, and Cadee appearing, Anna reaching for the meal in the oven, the younger men for the plates, Cadee for their beverages, coffee for most, tea for Devaney.

Chapter 29

Sitting back finally to watch the others, Devaney was surprised as the two younger men cleared the round oak table, putting away the food, loading the dishwasher, wiping off the table before straightening the woven placemats, and then sat back down. A frown on her face, she studied Blair, finding him watching her.

"We pray after a meal here, Devaney. No pressure on anyone. But that is what Doc and Anna do."

She shrugged. "Ok. I'm fine with that." She didn't see the surprised looks on the faces around her as she bowed her head.

Devaney rose after a while and walked to the office, her mind already sifting through what she needed to do. Blair watched her and then turned to Benen.

"What has she done?"

"I would suspect set up a database. Let's find your lady and see what she has done."

Blair stood behind Devaney, his arms around her, as he stared at the monitor. "Care to explain what you've been doing?"

She spun, shoving him down into the chair, a grin crossing his face as he remembered how many times she had done just that. "I need you to look this over. I have tried to think of everyone we knew, where we knew them from, how they might be related. That sort of thing. Please. Add to it." Turning to Benen, she stared at him for a moment. "When he's done, can you look it over? I need to start a search for anything that might be in common."

"I get you. I can do that." Benen watched as she paced before she abruptly left the room. He heard her footsteps heading for her bedroom and then sighed. Blair, this is not going to be easy. She's not letting anyone in, at least I don't think she is.

Cadee had been watching and followed Devaney, a tap at her open door before she walked in and sat with her.

"What? No words? Everyone needs to fill the silence, don't they?"

Cadee just smiled at the words. "No. No words. No platitudes. Just a friend sitting with a friend. Sometimes, that is all you need."

Devaney turned to her. "Is that what this is?"

"I would like to be your friend. You need us, and we need you."

"You do?" Devaney was surprised at her words.

"We do. Berneen and I would like to get to know you much better. Can we?" Cadee watched the other woman closely, finally seeing her nod. "But right now, you want silence. I can do that."

Blair finally stood, letting Benen have his place at the computer. Benen's fingers flew over the keyboard, before he sat back, a deep frown on his face before it cleared.

"Benen?"

"Blair, she's good. If she hasn't done this in a while, then she must have been really good at it once. We could use her where I work." He turned to look up and then rose. "It will take a while for this to work. She has made some interesting connections."

"I know she has. I don't see how." Blair paced before he turned to face Benen. "Will it help?"

"I'm sure it will. It certainly won't hurt." He paused, biting at his lip. "How are you really doing, Blair?"

Blair shrugged, not quite sure how to answer. "To tell you the truth, Benen, I am not sure. I have nothing to base what I'm feeling or seeing on."

Benen nodded. "The ladies do that to you. They get us all mixed up. That's a given with the ladies." He turned as he heard a chime from the computer. "It looks as if something has been found." He sat, bringing up the results, a frown on his face. "Blair?"

"What did you find?" Blair looked over his shoulder, surprise on his face. "Them?"

"Yeah. Them. I didn't know you knew them."

Blair shrugged. "I don't remember them. But Devaney has put them down for some reason."

Devaney spoke from beside him. "What did you find, Benen?"

He spun in the chair and then was on his feet, heading for the printer. "This. How do you know this couple?"

She stared at him and then at the paperwork. "Them? I'm not sure now. I just remembered their names and what they did." She paced, her eyes on the printed page, not hearing Blair speaking to her.

"Devaney?"

Devaney jumped as Blair's hand touched hers, and she looked up at him, fear in her face for a moment, causing him to frown and then sigh to himself. How do I do this, Lord? How do I approach her without scaring her?

"Blair? What is it?"

"Those names. I don't remember them. I'm not sure if I have even met them."

She shook her head. "I'm sure we did." She stared at him, her mind thinking back through the years. "At college. They were part of the leadership in the church, if I remember."

Blair's eyes slid closed. "They were, weren't they?" He turned to Benen. "We were part of a young adult group at church. We have, if I remember, four couples who sponsored us. This couple was one of them." He tapped the paper Devaney still held.

Devaney shoved the paper back at him. "Here, you take it. I don't want it anymore."

Blair grinned for a moment, passing the paper over to Benen. "Here, let Benen have it. He started it all."

Cadee began to laugh as Devaney and Blair stared at each other before their eyes turned to Benen, who stood, papers in his hand, his eyebrows raised, a look of almost shock on his face. He had not been prepared for Blair to do that. His eyes narrowed as he studied his friend and then his friend's lady before his eyes raised to his wife, causing Cadee to laugh even harder, bringing Doc and Anna to the door, questioning what was so funny.

Benen shook his head. "I'm getting blamed for this." He held up the papers. "Somehow, I don't think I did this." His eyes narrowed as he studied Devaney, seeing humour lurking in her eyes. "Devaney?"

She laughed. "Sorry, Benen. Blair does that. Didn't you know that?"

The others laughed as Blair protested that, saying it had only happened when he was a teenager, Devaney shaking her head at him.

Chapter 30

Blair was on a search that Saturday, not finding Devaney. He needed to talk to her. Will had been around, and Blair had given him the names they had come up with. He had looked at Blair, looked at the page, and then shook his head, asking why Devaney had started this, and did she not realize how much work she had just made for him? Blair had laughed, telling him he knew that, but did he know how much both he and Devaney wanted this over with? Will had shaken his head and told Blair to find Devaney. He wanted to speak with her.

Devaney raised her head from where she had it resting on her arm laying along the back of a bench. She had chosen to hide outside that day, the weather a bit warmer, but still cool. She didn't want Blair to find her, knowing right well he had questions for her. She had seen Will earlier and knew he had the same. She sighed to herself. Now what, Lord? I want to be free of this. I want to believe like I used to, to find You once more, but it just doesn't seem to be working.

Blair stood for a moment, his eyes on her, before he sat, an arm finally coming around her to pull her back against him. She waited, waited for what, she wasn't sure, but he didn't speak. His hand covered hers.

They sat, not speaking, the sounds of the morning in their ears. Devaney finally laid her head against Blair's arm, her free hand wrapping around his arm, before she spoke.

"Blair?"

"Yeah?" She could hear the hesitation in his voice, and shifted slightly in how she was sitting. His arm tightened around her before he spoke. "Will was looking for you."

"That doesn't sound good."

He laughed. "I gave him what we discovered. He said you made a lot of work for him."

She shook her head. "No, not really. If he looks at the ones we think are at fault, then it shouldn't be that much work."

Blair sat for a moment. "He'll look at them all. You know, I don't remember them."

"They were there, but I don't really remember much about them. Would our foster mom?"

"I sent her an email this morning. She's looking into finding a picture for us and any information that may help. She did say they are no longer there, that she had heard they moved east."

"Moved east? Like in where?" Devaney suddenly felt fear and turned more towards Blair. "Are they here? In this area?"

Blair shrugged. "Will said he'd look into that." His eyes raised at Bradon walked towards them.

"What does he want?" She sounded disgruntled, finding that she didn't want anyone else around them, she was content just to be held by Blair, with only his company.

———

Bradon sat at the other end of the bench, his eyes watching the birds as they fluttered around the feeders. Devaney kept her eyes on him, not realizing that Blair was watching her intently before his eyes raised to Bradon.

"Bradon? Shouldn't you be at work or volunteering or something?" Devaney finally spoke.

Bradon shook his head even as a grin broke out on his face. "It's Saturday, Devaney. I don't have anything on today."

She stared at him. "So, you just want to sit out here, in the cold, and watch us? Is that it?"

Bradon laughed before his attention was turned to the trees behind them, hearing a sound of footsteps that shouldn't be there.

"Devaney. Blair. Now. To the building."

Blair was on his feet, his hand pulling Devaney with him, as he ran towards the building, Bradon following. A sudden crack sounded through the air, and Devaney's hand flew to her head before she stumbled, her hand pulled for Blair's grip, and she tumbled to the ground. Bradon tackled Blair, taking him down, before he slid towards Devaney, fear on his face as he saw the blood on her head.

"Bradon?"

"Stay down, Blair. I'm not sure if they're done yet or not." He could see the men that were around exiting the building, running towards them. He shoved at Blair, moving him towards Branigan and Breck, before he scooped Devaney into his arms, heading as quickly as he could for the infirmary, shouting for Brady or Doc, one of them to come, Devaney was hurt.

Brady reached for Devaney, helping to settle her on the bed, his eyes narrowing as he assessed the wound.

"What happened?"

"She was shot. I heard something behind us, started them for the building, and then she was down." Bradon was angry, angry that Devaney was hurt, angry that he couldn't have prevented it, angry that this was happening to one more of them. God, where are You in this? What's the reason?

Doc was there, his eyes on Blair before he motioned him from the room. Blair fought them, not wanting to leave, his own eyes on Devaney, seeing just as Bradon had the blood on the side of her head. Lord, please. Don't take her from me now that I've found her again. I can't do this. He paced the hallway, Branigan keeping step with him, the other men mingling around them.

Barnabas stood and watched him, feeling like he had done this not too long ago. Will stood beside him.

"This is hurting him even more, Barnabas." Will's quiet comment barely broke the silence in the hallway.

"I know. I don't know how to make it better for him."

"We can't. Only God can. And He has allowed this for some reason." Will turned as an officer approached him. "No sign of the shooter?"

The officer shook his head. "Not much of a one. He was in and out quickly, we can tell, but there's not a lot of evidence. No shell casing. Nothing." He was frustrated.

"Keep searching. Let me know if you find anything." Will turned back to see Blair standing in the doorway, his eyes glued to the room, his face white.

Chapter 31

As Blair watched Doc and Brady, he could heard quiet, hurried words between them but was unable to make out what was being said. His eyes stayed focused on Devaney, not sure how she was. All he could see was blood, the bloody wipes they were using, the bandages they were pulling out. He could see they were rushing, but he just wished they would talk to him.

Baird pulled him to one side as he watched the paramedics coming down the hallway, almost on a run, the noise of the stretcher wheels loud in the silence surrounding them. He was afraid for his friend, for his friend's lady.

Branigan's hand was there to draw him away, to speak with Will. Will watched Blair closely, finally moving him away from the hallway and to the lobby.

"Blair? I know you want to be in there with her, but I need you to talk to me. What happened?"

Blair shook his head, his eyes focusing on Will. "I'm not really sure. We had been sitting out there. Bradon came out and then he was up and ordering us to run for the building. I didn't hear anything, just lost her hand as she fell. Bradon took me down and then the others were there, rushing me inside." He spun, his eyes towards the infirmary. "I need to get back there. I need to be with her."

Will's hand kept him in place. "They're working on her right now. She'll be heading into the hospital soon. We'll get you there." He paused, rubbing at his face. "Blair, I need your attention."

Blair's eyes focused on Will, a frown on his face. "My attention? Why?"

"That list? Could it be someone from it?"

Blair shrugged, his eyes studying Will. "Why would you think that?"

Will shrugged. "It just seems coincidental. That's all. We need to talk about that."

The younger man sighed, shoving his hands into his jacket pockets, his fingers on his keys as he rubbed at them. "How would they have know what we were working on? You didn't get it until this morning." He spun as he heard the stretcher heading his way and was gone before Will could stop him.

Barnabas shook his head, walking rapidly towards Blair, his eyes meeting Breck, who nodded, heading for the outdoors and a vehicle. He watched as Blair's hands reached for Devaney, his hand on hers as she was moved quickly towards the ambulance. His hand came out to stop him from climbing aboard.

"Breck will take you, Blair." He waited for Blair to respond, even as the doors were shut on the ambulance, and it raced away, leaving a white-faced devastated Blair standing, watching before he turned.

"What did you say?"

"Breck's here. He'll take you. Branigan's here as well. Go with them. We'll meet you there."

Blair finally nodded, his feet slow to move him forward towards the truck, Branigan's hand on his arm.

Will shook his head. "I'll have patrol follow them. There will be someone at the hospital when they get there." He sighed, his eyes searching the area. "Someone's out there, Barnabas."

"I know. I can feel them." He looked around. "Do you need any of us? They'll all want to go."

"Go ahead." He nodded towards the building. "Your security's here. We'll call you if we need to."

Blair paced the gray and white tiled floor in the Emergency Department waiting room, not see the various plants and pictures around the area. His sole focus was the door to the examination rooms, where Devaney was. He had no idea how she was, if she was even alive. His hands jammed into his pockets, he made tour after tour of the room, moving around those walking there and around the chairs and tables. He know his friends were there but he couldn't speak. He didn't see Buckley pacing with him on one side and Baird on the other.

His friends exchanged glances as they gathered, Anna arriving with Cadee and Berneen, their voices hushed, their faces white and worried. Doc had arrived, his feet carrying him to where Devaney was, his eyes assessing her, his hands reaching to help. He followed as she was taken for imaging and X-rays, not willing to let her out of his sight. He knew the staff, knew she was being taken care of.

He stepped back finally as the surgeon on call examined her, his thoughts muddled for a moment.

Devaney, for some reason, had taken a part of both his and Anna's hearts, without realizing she had done so. He wanted her to be well, to walk out of there, but he knew she wouldn't.

The surgeon stepped back, his eyes assessing Devaney, before he turned to the physician treating her.

"Do you know a health history for her?"

Doc spoke up. "She's a new friend to us, Tom. But Blair may know something. I did blood work a bit ago after she was found in the woods near our place. She had been run off the road. It showed she was somewhat anemic."

Tom Grafton's eyes studied Doc, before he nodded. "And how is she related to Blair? I thought he was an orphan."

"He is. She was in the same foster home as he was out in Alberta. Apparently they are engaged, but he never said a word. She's been making her way across the country by stages, from what she said."

"Let's get him in here. He wasn't hurt?"

"Not this time." Doc hesitated. "They were run down a day or so after Devaney reappeared. Blair had a broken tibia but it's healed."

Tom shook his head. "What next! Can't these young people find some other way to have fun?"

Chapter 32

Feeling a hand on his shoulder, Blair turned from where he was standing at the window, staring out at the parking lot, his hand coming out to brace himself against a pillar. Doc stood there, a closed look on his face, before he nodded at Tom.

"Blair, this is Tom Grafton. He's a surgeon called in to treat, Devaney."

"Dr. Grafton? How is she?" Blair was almost afraid to ask, as desperate as he was for word.

"We're still assessing her, Blair. There are imaging results to come." His hand reached for Blair's arm, turning him towards the examination rooms. "Come, let's get you into your lady. Before you go in, you understand that she was shot, the bullet creasing the side of her head. We are waiting to see if there are any fractures or bleeding in the brain. That we would need to treat."

Blair nodded, not quite understanding or hearing what they were saying to him. His whole focus was getting to Devaney. "She's alive?"

"She is, Blair. That she is. We'll have to wait until she awakes to fully assess her." Doc's hand on his shoulder guided him towards the cubicle she was in, Buckley's footsteps keeping pace with them.

Blair hesitated at the doorway, his eyes raised upwards as he prayed, his heart flooding with tears.

He walked forward, Doc's arm on his shoulder for support, to stand, his eyes searching the equipment surrounding Devaney before they sought her face. He drew in a deep breath, seeing her pallor, the blood still evident where it had not been washed away, the beginning of bruising showing, the large white bandage that surrounded her head. He reached for a hand, finding hers cold and lifeless and limp. His heart tried to pray, but he had no words.

His eyes traced her beloved features, seeing the pain etched in them before his hand reached to touch her face. He looked up at Doc and then the surgeon.

"Doc?"

Doc shook his head. "I'm not the one treating her, Blair. Tom is and then there's the other emergency physician. They'll talk to you."

Blair nodded, his eyes back on his beloved Devaney, not hearing Buckley as he prayed for them and those treating her. He was finally moved back and to the waiting room, his head turning to watch her for as long as he could.

Will stood in front of him. "Blair?"

"Will, don't even ask another question." Blair walked away, anger on his face, his mind whirling with what had happened. He hit the exit door and paced the parking lot, finally realizing he wasn't alone.

Baird, Benen, Bradon, Brady and Branigan paced with him. He could see the other men watching from the sidewalk, Doc standing with them, Anna, Berneen and Cadee there as well.

"Why?"

"Why what?" Branigan answered his question with a question.

"Why her? Why shoot her? Where is God in this? How did He allow this?"

The men with him exchanged glances before studying his face even as they paced through the parking lot.

Baird finally spoke, his eyes searching the sky overhead for answers, watching the clouds scudding by. "He is here, Blair. She could be dead, but she's not. He has her in the hollow of His hand."

Blair shook his head. "I know that, Baird. I just want to know why. Why her? Who is it that's after her?"

Branigan shared a look with Benen, knowing what they had worked on the night before. "Can we get a list of the names you came up with? Benen said Devaney had set up a database and searched it."

Baird came to an abrupt halt, his hands scrubbing down his face. He finally nodded. "Doc or Anna can get it for you. Unless...". His words died away for a moment. "Benen, you took a copy?"

"I did. I'll pass it on to the guys. Will has it and said he was working through it." He gave a small smile that didn't reach his eyes. "He does need to talk to you, Blair. That's why he was out there this morning."

Blair sighed. "I know. I didn't want to talk to him. Nor did Devaney." He turned to study the hospital, not seeing Will standing hear him. "I have an email out to our foster parents about one of the couples. She was looking for more information for us, but she did say they had moved east. I wonder if they're in this province."

Will spoke, causing Blair's eyes to slide shut before he turned. "Which couple?"

Blair just shook his head, heading back inside, leaving them all standing and staring after him.

"Benen?"

Will's question brought his head around and Benen sighed. "I'm not sure which one. They were talking about three or four, I think."

"Can you remember which ones?"

Benen shook his head. "I would have to ask Blair, and I'm not prepared to do that right now." He walked away, leaving a frustrated Will behind him.

"Give them some time, Will. Blair needs that. So do the rest of the men." Doc stood beside him. "With what they've gone through with Baird and Benen, and now this, it makes them wonder which one of them will be next."

"That's what I am afraid of, Doc. That's it will be them all."

Chapter 33

His eyes on the ICU doors, Blair stood, his hands jammed into his jeans pockets, not moving, waiting to be let into where Devaney lay. He heard the quiet conversations behind him. The men had all come to him, prayed for him and Devaney and then left. Other than Barnabas, Bradon and Buckley. He knew they wouldn't. Bradon had connected with Devaney for some reason, he thought, just as Branigan had. Benen had commented that he was going home to research the names, and just what ones did he want him to pass on to Will. Blair had stared at him and then just shrugged, stating he really didn't care at that point.

Doc watched him before he approached, just standing with him, no words necessary. He prayed for his young friends, knowing that Anna had contacted their church family, setting the prayer chain to work. He had receiving multiple texts from the men and women there, asking for updates as he could, just letting him know the young couple were prayed. for.

"Doc?" Blair's voice was broken and barely audible. "How is she? Really?"

"How is she? Lucky to be alive, Blair."

"I know that, Doc. But what are we facing? I can't lose her, not now. Not when I've just found her again."

Neither man saw the woman standing in the waiting room, her eyes full of hatred on Blair. She finally turned and walked away, her fingers busy on her phone, before a man appeared, standing where she had, watching Blair closely.

Blair finally moved forward, through the doors that swung closed quietly behind him, his eyes on the nurse who had come to find him. She smiled, pointing to a cubicle.

"In there, Blair. You can stay for a while. We'll be in and out. Dr. Grafton said he'd be around in a bit." She looked at Doc, who nodded.

Blair stood for a moment, before he entered the room, his thoughts muddled, knowing he needed to pray, but his mind just could not form the words. Please, dear Lord? He felt Doc's hand on his shoulder once more, heard his prayer, and then looked towards the bed.

He took in the medical equipment around Devaney, knowing it was necessary, but hating that hit had to be there. He moved forward, his sneakers squeaking on the tiled floor, before he stood, his hands clenching and unclenching, tears flooding his eyes and blinding him for a moment before he blinked rapidly and turned to study his lady.

His hand reached for hers, holding it tightly, feeling it warmer than it had been. His attention turned to her face and his free hand laid against her cheek, seeing her flinch at his touch, causing a frown to appear on his face. He turned as he heard footsteps stop near the bed.

Dr. Grafton studied Blair before he moved up beside Devaney, assessing her, his eyes watching the monitors, before, a penlight in his hand, he checked her pupil reaction.

"Dr. Grafton? How is she?"

"Lucky to be alive, Blair." The surgeon stood, his hands on the bedrail, his eyes on Blair. "I guess you could say God was watching for her today. It could have been much worse."

"She could be dead."

Dr. Grafton nodded. "She could be. Or the damage could be much worse. We have the imaging studies back. There is no fracture. There is no brain bleed, and I don't expect there to be one. However, she is far from out of the woods."

Blair nodded. "I didn't think she was. What are we facing? How long before she's awake?"

Dr. Grafton shook his head. "At this point, I am not sure what we are facing with her. As to that, we can't properly assess her until she's awake and coherent. There was concern about her eyes, whether there was swelling around the optic nerves. There isn't. But as to what she is facing when she awakes, we'll talk. We'll talk about what she's facing and what you're facing with her." He studied the younger man. "I am assuming you're not walking away from her."

Blair stood for a moment, shocked at the words, then shook his head. "I had too many years without her. I won't walk away from her, not ever. I don't know what I'd do if she did that to me again."

Doc shook his head at the other physician, knowing they'd talk, and he'd have to share what had transpired with the two in front of them.

His hand on Blair's arm once more, Doc led him from the room, back to where they could find chairs to sit. He sat, a sigh drawn from him, knowing that Blair would be back with Devaney as soon as he could. His eyes met Buckley's questioning ones before he shook his head.

"Blair?"

Blair finally looked around, his eyes shadowed. "Doc? What are her chances? Will she awake?"

"Right now, I don't know. I won't lie to you, Blair. You know me better than that. As for her chances, we can't fully assess her, as Tom explained, while she's unconscious. We can do limited testing, make educated guesses, give you those. But somehow, that's not what you want or what you're asking."

Blair shook his head, his eyes on his hands he was rubbing together. "It's not, Doc. It's not that. I just don't know what I'll face, or what she'll face. I don't even know if she'll stay with me. And I just want the person responsible to be found and face the consequences."

"We know you do, Blair. We all want that for you two." Buckley's voice had his head swinging that way. "We have you covered in prayer, Blair, both of you."

"Thank you, Buckley. I assume the prayer chain is at work."

"Anna's got it going. Benen was going over the list and was to speak with Will."

Blair nodded once more, his phone in his head. "I just heard from my foster mom. That couple is in this area. How did they find me? I didn't tell anyone other than my foster parents where I was moving to."

"Then, we will need to give their names to Will. He'll need to look into them, just as a matter of course, you do know that, Blair." Buckley's eyes showed the sadness he was feeling for his friends.

"I know, Buckley. I know. I just wish it was different."

Chapter 34

Four days later, Blair stood once more beside Devaney, his hands on hers, as he watched her head begin to toss and turn, pain on her face as she started to rouse. He had been warned it would not be pretty when that happened, that he could expect her to rouse and then sleep.

He waited, a sigh rising within him, followed by prayers, as he watched her struggle to awake, lose the battle, and then struggle again. It had been going on all day. He was fatigued, no, he thought, bone-deep weary, and he just wanted her to wake up, so he could tell her he loved her and didn't want to lose her, that he wanted her to be by his side for life.

Devaney's eyes finally stayed open, and she blinked, a frown appearing on her face, as she stared at the ceiling, not sure where she was or even why. She jumped as she felt a hand touch her hand and then her face. Her head turned and she blinked again, sighing as she saw Blair.

"Blair? Where am I?" She had to clear her throat to make the words audible.

"You're in the hospital, Devaney."

She continued to frown at him. "Blair, you don't look the same. You need to shave." Her eyes searched the room, a headache making it difficult to see. Her hand reached for her head, Blair's hand stopping it.

"Blair?" She questioned him, and then her eyes slid closed, and she slept, Blair's heart breaking for his lady.

Dr. Grafton had stopped in the doorway as he heard their voices before he walked forward.

"She's been awake?"

Blair nodded. "Just briefly. I don't think she knows exactly where she is. And I don't think she knows what year it is."

"Why would you say that?"

"Just the way she looked at me. She told me I didn't look the same. That tells me she's missing some years." He blinked rapidly, his heart breaking for his lady even as he prayed for recovery for her.

Dr. Grafton nodded. "We spoke of that, Blair, that she may have memory loss. Whether it's permanent or not, we will have to wait to see." He held up a hand, a small smile on his face, as he studied the younger man. "I know, Blair. You want her awake and the same as she was. That may never happen. You have been told that."

"I know. I do know that. It's just so hard, to see her like this, knowing someone tried to kill her and not know who or why."

"Will has not said anything?"

Blair shook his head. "I haven't talked to him since Devaney was admitted. I can't. He just says they're working on it."

Dr. Grafton's head turned as he heard footsteps and saw Will and a woman he knew to be a detective waiting at the door. "Will's here, Blair. Come. Let's get you out to speak with him. We need to assess your lady anyway."

Blair turned reluctantly before he turned back, bending to kiss Devaney's forehead, a hand resting on her cheek, a prayer rising for her complete healing. He blinked, not wanting the men to see him weep, before he raised her hand to kiss that, tucking it back under the blanket. He turned once more, straightened his shoulders and walked towards Will, knowing somehow that when Will spoke, it would change his life and that of his lady.

Will watched compassion in his eyes even as Bridget Green waited to speak with Blair. She was the detective assigned to his case and needed to question him and then bring him up to date on their findings. Will had already warned her that Blair would not like what she had found.

"Blair?" Will's voice was soft. "Have you eaten today?"

Blair stopped, not sure if he had. "I don't think I have, Will."

"Then, come. Let's find the cafeteria and get some food into you." He nodded towards Bridget. "This is Detective Bridge Green. She needs to speak with you. But first, we need to eat."

Chapter 35

His head bowed, Blair stared down at his tray of food, not really hungry but knowing Devaney would ask him to eat. He picked up his sandwich, laid it back down, and instead reached for the cup of coffee he had chosen. Will watched him closely, seeing the fatigue weighing his young friend down and knowing that when Bridget spoke to him, it would be even worse for him.

Will shook his head before he spoke. "Eat, Blair. Then, we'll talk. We do need to do that."

Blair nodded, reaching for his sandwich, his thoughts in the ICU with Devaney, before he finally pushed away his tray, not realizing he had eaten the meal he had on it. His hands wrapped around his mug, his eyes on Will.

"So, Will, where do we stand with this?"

Will nodded his head towards Bridget. "She'll update you. But I must say that the work Devaney did with her database was helpful."

"It was? We wondered if it would be. She was good at this at school."

Bridget spoke. "She has helped." She paused, not quite sure how to proceed, never having spoken to Blair before.

"Spit it out, Detective. I need to get back up to Devaney."

Bridget stared at him for a moment. "Okay. So, the couple you narrowed a list down to? We spoken to them. They are moving back to Alberta. They didn't know you were here."

Blair shook his head. "That's not happening. They can say what they want, but they knew. I've realized I've seen them here in town, found them watching me. So, go back to them and confront them. If I remember correctly, none of the young adults cared for them much. There were rumours about what they were involved in back there. Have you spoken to anyone there?"

"Not as yet. I didn't feel a need to." Bridget was becoming defensive.

Blair stood, his eyes on her, before he spoke. "I won't talk to her anymore, Will. I'll talk to you. I'll talk to another detective. To have this conversation? To have our concerns swept away, especially when someone just tried to kill my fiancee? Not happening again. And don't tell me it's our foster parents. I know that's what the thought is. It's not them. You wouldn't even consider it if you knew them." He turned as he heard his name called, his face whitening for a moment before he was across the room, hugging the older woman who stood there before hugging the man with her, turning to walk away with them.

Will shook his head at Bridget. "Did you not speak with anyone back in their home town?"

Bridget stared at him. "I didn't think I needed to. They were upfront with me."

Will sighed. "No, that's not how we do things. You know better. I am going to have to ask that you be removed from this. I need someone who can work with them. And Blair won't work with you, not after this. You don't have his trust in you, and you need that." He rose and walked away, leaving Bridget staring after him, before her phone was out and she was sending a text. She rose, walking away, not seeing an officer following her on Will's instructions. He waited as she met with a couple and then walked away. His own head shook as he recognized who they were. He just knew Will would not like this.

Chapter 36

Blair turned from the window in the waiting room, his eyes searching for their foster mother. He had not expected the couple to leave their home and fly out here, but they had. Joseph and Ellen Liscombe had been there for both of them when they were teenagers. He had felt their prayers over the years, missing her hugs and words of encouragement each day, his words of well done and why can't you.

"Blair?" Ellen moved towards him. "How is Devaney?"

He shrugged. "We're not too sure as yet. I told you she was shot. She was awake earlier, but I'm not sure how well she is. She seems to have lost a few years."

"I'm sure she has." Joseph spoke from beside him. "It would be reasonable to expect that. Listen, can we get in to see her?"

Blair nodded. "Of course. She'll not expect you." He looked around. "Do you have somewhere to stay?"

Joseph shook his head. "That wasn't important for us. You and Devaney are."

Barnabas spoke from behind them, startling the older couple. "We have a guest suite you are welcome to use."

The older couple spun, their eyes on Barnabas, even as Blair smiled.

"This is my employer, Barnabas Carey. He's right.   There is a suite you can use.   Thank, Barnabas."

Late that night, Blair stood at his window. Doc had made him come home, told him that he needed to, that Devaney would want him to. He hadn't liked that, but he knew Doc was thinking about him and worried about him.

Blair turned, a frown on his face. He was unsure about something, and just what that was, he didn't know. His frown deepened as he thought about the detective and realized that's what was puzzling him. She didn't seem to be doing the work she should have been doing, he thought. I need to talk to Will and see where the investigation really lies.

He pulled out his phone, reading the text from Will, knowing he would find him the next day. Walking through his apartment, he searched, looking for what he was not sure, but he knew he was looking for something. Finally stretching out on the couch, his eyes closed as he prayed and then slept, the early morning light awakening him. Sitting up, Blair rubbed at his eyes and then reached for his phone, afraid to check for any messages. There were none, especially not from the hospital, and that was good, he thought.

Showered, shaved, dressed in clean clothes, Blair drove away from the building, not noticing that Branigan and Baird stood watching him, before they were in Branigan's truck following him. They didn't want him on his own and had no way of knowing why. The two men stood in the waiting room, watching as Blair moved silently towards Devaney's room, eager to see his beloved.

Blair stood beside her bed, watching as she moved restlessly, not sure of anything anymore. He needed answers that weren't forthcoming. He frowned as he thought of his foster parents making the trip to be with them. That is not what he had expected. Now, that other couple? Where were they?

He watched Devaney closely, his hand on her cheek, as her eyelids fluttered and then she relaxed again. His hand was on hers, feeling hers turning to grip his.

"Blair? Is that you?" Her eyes finally opened, searching the room before she focused on him. "Where am I? My head hurts."

"You're in the hospital, love. You have been for a few days."

"I have? I don't remember. Where are we?"

"We're in a hospital in Ontario."

"Ontario? When did we come here? Aren't we supposed to be getting married on Saturday? Did I miss graduation?"

"No, you didn't miss it." He sighed, his hand tightened on hers. "We need to talk, Devaney. You're not remembering a few years."

"I'm not? How come?"

"Because someone shot at you, trying to kill you. You were hit in the head."

Her eyes were huge as she stared at him. "Let me sit up."

"Not yet. You can't. They want you laying flat for a few more days."

She pulled her hand from his, reaching for the controls, raising the bead of the bed slightly. "Now, why did I do that?" Her head pounded for a few minutes until the pain subsided somewhat.

"That's what they didn't want." Blair sat on the edge of the bed. "What is the last you remember?"

"Us walking towards the library." Her brow wrinkled. "No, that's not it. It's a building I don't recognize. Why don't I?"

Blair's phone was out and he pulled up a picture of the Barnabas Foundation Building. "Is this the one?"

She squinted at it. "It is. You said it's not Alberta."

"No, it's not. You walked away from me back in Alberta. I have work with the Barnabas Foundation. Somehow you made your way across the country and found me, but it took years."

"Years?" Her voice rose to a squeak. "It can't have. What year is it?"

When he told her, she frowned at him. "It can't be."

"Sorry, my love. It is. We're in the middle of what we call an adventure. We need to talk about that, but not right now." Blair looked back at the door. "Our foster parents are here."

"They are? Why?"

"To see you. I let them you know you were hurt. You know how they are."

Devaney frowned before she looked up at him. 'They're not the ones, are they?"

"The ones, who?"

"The ones who have been following me. I know someone has been. I just don't know who. Why can't I remember?"

"Dr. Grafton, your surgeon, says you might not remember everything or you might. He wants to talk to you now that you're awake and coherent." He grinned at her frown. "You've lost some years. We don't know if you will ever get them back."

Her head went back on the pillow. "I can see someone standing watching me, Blair, but I don't know who. I should know him, but I can't remember. Why not?"

"You've buried everything deep in order to survive. I'll have Will, the police chief, come and talk to you." He frowned as he remembered the detective. "There was a detective, a Bridget Green, but she seemed to think our foster parents were the ones after you. We have figured out another couple, but she didn't think it was them. She said she spoke with them and was confident it wasn't."

"She didn't do her research, did she?"

"No, I don't think she did. She didn't contact anyone back there." He paused. "Do you remember the names we came up with?"

She shrugged. "Not that I know of." Her eyes slid closed and she slept, leaving Blair standing staring at her before he shook his head.

Devaney, what am I to do with you, he thought. How do we go on? You don't remember what happened, and I need you to.

He turned as he felt someone standing beside him. Will had appeared.

"She's been awake?"

Blair nodded. "She has. She doesn't remember much though. She thinks we're still just finishing college and then she's jumping to the present."

Will shrugged, concern on his face. "I suspect that's what she'll be doing." He turned to watch Blair. "I hear your foster parents are in town."

"They are. They took vacation time to come east. I would have told them not to." Blair's head went down. "And you want to talk to them."

Will shook his head. "I have already. They approached me yesterday. Barnabas put them in touch with me."

"And do you think they would do this?"

"No, I don't. And now we can't find Bridget."

"Bridget? What's her last name?"

Will spun as Devaney spoke. "Green. Why?"

"Because there was a Bridget Green in some of my classes. Do you have a picture of her?"

"I can get one to you later. Why would you say that?"

“Because she wasn't who she pretended to be.” Horror grew on her face. “Blair! That couple! She's related to them!”

Chapter 37

Will walked back towards Blair as he sat in the waiting room, his eyes on Will. The older man sank to a seat, a sigh coming from him. Blair waited, knowing that Will would speak when he was ready.

"How's Devaney this afternoon?"

Blair shrugged. "A bit better. She's being moved from ICU tomorrow."

"And you'll be able to be with her during visiting hours only. I hear you, Blair."

"I know. Being engaged to her doesn't seem to make a difference."

"But being married would?" Will watched as Blair spun on his seat, his eyes on his friend.

"Just what are you suggesting?"

"That you marry Devaney. That way, you can stay all the time. We'll make those arrangements."

Blair sat back. "I've thought of that. I just don't know if she's ready to do that."

"She is. I've watched her. She's still in love with you, regardless of what she has said."

Blair finally nodded. "I need to talk to her." He looked up as Buckley sat beside him. "Buckley?"

"Don't wait. I heard what Will asked you. She's ready or rather, she was."

———

Blair nodded. "All we can say is to ask her. See what she says."

An hour later, Devaney stared at Blair, her mouth opening and closing. "You want to do what?"

"I asked if you would still marry me, today." He shoved his hands through his hair, pacing the room before he stood in front of her. "Forget it, Devaney. I know you're not ready, no matter what others say."

"Blair?" At her quiet voice, he paused in his walk away from her and came back, to stand, his eyes on her. "Maybe we should."

He shook his head. "I'm not sure, love. I don't want you to commit that way and then find out you made a mistake."

"It's no mistake, Blair. You said I ran from you all those years ago. Maybe, if I hadn't, I wouldn't be here in this hospital bed." She pointed at the door. "Get what you need. You say you have a minister friend?"

"I do. Buckley. He'll do the ceremony." Blair stood, his heart wanting to take this step, to keep his beloved safe, but he still wasn't sure. He prayed for peace, but didn't find it. At least, not the way he thought he would.

Devaney watched Blair walk out of the room, her head sinking back as her eyes closed. Lord, is this You? Are You leading us? Or are we rushing into something neither one of is sure we even want anymore? I know he still has my heart, he always will. He says he loves me, but he stays back from me, as if he's just saying the words, but isn't committed anymore. How do we do this? How do I do this? Lord, I know You're here. Please, Lord, give both us of peace about this.

Hearing the door open, she looked up to see Anna standing there before she walked over to stand beside her, reaching to hug the younger woman. Her head pounding as she moved, Devaney clung to the older woman.

"Devaney, what have you two gone and done?" Anna's quiet question finally broke the silence.

"We've decided to get married. Should we?" Devaney looked everywhere but at Anna.

Anna's arm rested around Devaney as she prayed for wisdom. "What does your heart say, Devaney?"

"It says to." She looked up, tears blinding her for a moment. "I asked Blair if I hadn't walked away all those years ago, would this have happened?"

"We don't know that, dear. It may have. It may not have. We have a young friend, who went through an adventure but his favourite saying is that God has a plan and purpose we don't know about yet."

"He's right, isn't he?" She looked up at Anna. "Oh, Anna, what did I do?"

"You did what you felt was right at the time. You were afraid for Blair." She hugged the younger woman and then stood back. "Now, we have to do something about this."

"About what?" Devaney looked around. "What is we have to do?"

“We need to get you all spruced up, as my father used to say. Let me call Cadee or Berneen. They’ll help us.”

Blair watched Devaney closely that evening knowing it had been an emotional day for her. He sighed. This is not how he had planned to marry her. Not with her in a hospital bed, recovering from a gunshot, her mind fading back and forth between years. He saw how she was playing with her rings, and reached for her hand, stopping her movement.

Devaney watched as Blair's hand reached for hers and then heard his prayer. She realized just how much she had missed that. She hesitated before she spoke.

"She was around today, wasn't she?"

"Who?"

"Bridget. I know she was. I thought I heard her voice outside the room this afternoon."

Blair stared down at her before he looked towards the door. "It's possible. Will said he hadn't been able to find her. And that worries him."

"Of course, it would. It always does, doesn't it? She'll come find us when we least expect her, take us somewhere we can't escape from, and put our friends in danger. That's how it always works in books and movies."

Blair gave a low laugh. "It does. Now, the nurses will be in to settle you for the night. I'll be in the waiting room. They won't let me stay for long. You're tired and need to rest."

Devaney's eyes were on his face, watching him intently. "I know, and so do you. Can't Doc just take me back to the building? He has an infirmary he could use."

"He's talked about that. Or having you stay with Anna and him. But now, you'll be staying with me." He bit at his lip. "I'm sorry, Devaney. I'm sorry you won't have the pictures and memories."

She carefully shook her head. "They're not important." She stopped. "Blair, is that what this is about? To stop us from getting married? Who hates us that much?"

Blair stared down at her, seeing the agitation in her face. "What makes you say that?"

She shrugged, her eyes on him. "We have nothing of value, except one another. What if someone wanted to break us up, make us turn to someone else? Did we even consider that?"

Blair groaned. "I didn't. I'm not sure anyone else did." His phone was out and he sent a swift text off to Branigan. "Let me ask the guys. I know they're trying to work through this, but we're missing a piece of information. You said Bridget Green was in some of your classes. I don't really remember her, but what if she's the one?"

"I think she is. Have our foster parents left yet?"

He nodded. "They flew back out tonight. We can call or email them about this. They may have an idea as well." He looked around as the door opened. "It's time for you to sleep, love. I'll be back in later."

———

Blair stood outside her door, wanting to stay there, but knowing he needed to be away from her, to think. Her question had puzzled him but made him realize that just maybe she had come to the right conclusion. He sank down into a chair, his eyes on the floor, not seeing the man sitting across from him, watching, a cruel look in his eyes.

His eyes finally closed as he slept, his sleep disturbed by dreams. He eventually rose midway through the night and made his way to Devaney's room, pulling a chair to the side of the bed and reaching for her hand, watching as she slept, his mind wandering to their conversation the evening before. He groaned as he thought through their friends. There had been one young man, he thought a friend of Bridget's, who had keep his eye on Devaney, a look on his face that had scared Blair. How had he forgotten him? And now he had to get the name to Will. No, he thought, I'll give it to Branigan. They'll search him out. I know they will.

Lord, can we end this and soon? I need my lady safe, and right now she isn't. I thank You that she's finding her way back to believing in You. I know she always did, but she wandered, out in the desert for years. Thank You that You never let her wander far from You.

He felt Devaney's hand tighten on his and he looked up, finding her still sleeping, but needing that touch with him. He sighed. Where do we go from here? How do we keep her safe? Has she been the target all along, or has it been me? I can't get a clear grasp on that.

Blair looked up as he heard footsteps, and watched the nurse closely, watching that Devaney was not harmed, that she was taken care of. He knew, somehow, that taking the step they had, they had placed themselves in more danger. But he just didn't know from whom? And just how could he protect his beloved if he didn't know who was out there?

Chapter 39

Two days later, Blair carried Devaney into their apartment, hesitating as he watched her face, not sure where she wanted to be. Devaney was avoiding his look, staring around at what was now her home, not sure herself of where she wanted to be.

Blair sighed to himself. "Where would you like to be, love? The bedroom? The living room?"

She looked up at him and then stared down the hall, an uncertain look on her face. "What I would really like is a shower? Is that even possible?" She looked over his shoulder as a tap came at the door.

Anna entered, her eyes assessing first Blair and then Devaney. "I know exactly where you want to be. A shower. Blair? If you can help her to the bathroom, we'll get her cleaned up. And while we're doing that, she can decide where she wants to be. Your bandage is fine, Devaney. Doc will be along in a bit to change it for you."

Blair walked away, heading for the kitchen, reaching for the coffee carafe. He needed coffee and good coffee. The hospital coffee really didn't cut it, he thought. He then reached for the kettle, knowing Devaney would want her tea. At least, he thought she would.

Turning as he heard a voice, he stared at Doc and Will as they stood there, Branigan and Barnabas behind them.

"Coffee ready yet?" Doc grinned at him. "It's okay if it isn't. We can wait."

Blair nodded. "I just made it so it won't take long. What did you find out? You're all not here for my health, that I can tell. Doc, Devaney will need her bandage changed. Anna's helping her get cleaned up."

"Anna mentioned that. We'll look after it. But first, what can we do for you?" Doc's compassionate eyes watched Blair closely.

"Solve this. Let us figure out who it is. Will?"

Will pointed to a chair. "Sit, Blair. We'll pray and then talk. Perhaps by that time, Devaney will be out here and we can talk to you both together."

Devaney hesitated as she heard male voices and then turned to the living room, Anna at her side.

"I think I'll just stay here, Anna. I feel like I've run a marathon." Her hand was on her head, knowing she needed to take the pain pills she had been given but not wanting that. "Who is all here?"

"Doc, Will, Barnabas, Branigan. They're praying right now. They'll move here to talk to you. Have you remembered anything else?"

Devaney started to shake her head and stopped, not wanting the pain to worsen. "I don't know if I have."

Blair stood for a moment, a small tray in his hands with Devaney's tea and some toast, before he set it on the end table, and then shifted her over enough to sit beside her and then wrap her back into his arms, the blanket she was covered with pulled up over her. She tilted her head back to watch him, not aware of the looks they were garnering from the other five.

"Devaney?" Doc's voice brought her eyes to him. "I know I've changed your bandage, but you won't say how you're feeling."

"I'm not sure how I am to be. My head hurts. Someone is chasing either me or Blair or both of us. I want this over."

"We know you both do." Will set his mug of coffee down, pulling over a folder he had set down. "We've been looking into things. There is a new detective assigned to your case, and he's digging in backgrounds, including both of yours. It is standard that we do. From what we have seen, Bridget did not do that. We still can't find her."

"And if you can't find her, we are still at risk, aren't we?" Devaney's head went back on Blair's shoulder as he watched her closely. "When will this be over?"

"We're working on it, Devaney." Will searched her face before looking up at Blair. "We need to run some things by you. And of course, by Blair, as well." He hesitated as he studied them, not knowing them well enough to know how they'd react.

"What do you have, Will?" Blair's head went back slightly as his eyes narrowed, sudden fatigue hitting him.

"First, let me preface it by saying how sorrow I am it has taken all these years to come to light, Devaney. I know you felt you had no choice. That is alway how the victims have felt. None of us fault you

———

for what you did. This time, don't run, no matter how much you feel like it, and you will. Dallas, the detective, is working hard on tracking down these culprits. I have always told him he is like a terrier - never gives up on what he's after. You two need that. This had taken enough of your lives. I know why you did what you did, Blair, and why you felt you two had to marry so quickly. Well, maybe not so quickly." He paused to grin at the laughter his words brought.

He sipped his coffee, trying to organize his thoughts, without too much success. He opened the folder and then closed it, handing it over to Blair.

"What's this?" Blair was puzzled, studying the folder even as Devaney's hand came out to open it.

"It's where we stand right now. Dallas should be here to talk to you, but he's flown out to Alberta to follow up on some leads."

"He has?" Devaney shared a look with Blair and sighed, the sigh seemingly drawn from her toes upwards. "Then, we have more names for him to search into out there."

Will nodded. "I thought you might." He nodded towards the folder. "Look through that. Dallas is keeping me updated as he goes along. We are searching for that couple."

Devaney tilted her head back to look up at Blair, a frown on her face. "I think they are related somehow to Bridget? And there was a guy who hung around her. Do you remember him, Blair?"

"I do. Jerry Walsh."

Chapter 40

Devaney wandered the apartment that evening, not ready to settle down, not ready to stay up. This is so unlike me, she thought, to be so unsettled. I guess I'm entitled, with all that I have gone through. I don't have to like it. She turned as she heard Blair behind her, to find him watching her, a shuttered look on his face.

"Blair?"

"We need to talk, Devaney, about what Will gave us. I know we've looked it over, but there is something missing there. I'm not sure what." He turned as he heard a tap at the door and looked over at the clock.

Benen and Branigan stood inside the door, sharing looks, before Benen spoke.

"That list you gave me? I had copied her database and continued to run it. I found more names as I expanded the parameters." He looked up as Devaney peeked around Blair at him.

"More names? Is Will going to like this?"

Benen grinned at her. "He has them. He didn't say anything, but I think he recognized one."

"He did? Who?" Blair turned Devaney back to the kitchen, making her sit and then reaching to make her a cup of tea, even as Branigan poured coffee for the men.

"Whiteside. Dixon."

Her eyes grew round. "Them? Why?"

"He didn't say, but he indicated he'd be talking to you two again and asked if you could please stop throwing names at him. He was going to call Dallas, I think he said, as well."

"Dallas is the new detective." Blair paced, his hand on his face, before Devaney's hand on his arm stopped him.

"Blair, sit. There's more that they want to say."

"There is, Devaney." Benen eyed her and then Blair. "Will said to warn you that he's had word Bridget is still in the area. She's with a man, but he didn't know who."

The young couple exchanged a glance, even as Devaney rubbed at her forehead, the headache making it difficult to think.

"She'll be with Jerry Walsh. He's one she hung around with when we were in college. I used to see him watching Blair at times."

"You did? You never said anything?" Blair's arm was around her.

"He wasn't there a lot. Not enough to be concerned about. I just didn't feel comfortable when he was. Neither was Bridget there a lot." She sighed. "I just don't get why."

"Burnie had a theory. You know him, Blair. Always coming up with plots and scenes for his work." Branigan took pity on Devaney. "He's an author, Devaney. I know you've met them all, but you haven't yet found out what all they do."

"No, I haven't. But what is his theory?"

Once more Branigan's eyes studied the couple. "He thinks Bridget wants you out of the way. She wants to be his wife. And for you, Blair? Walsh wants you out of the way to get to Devaney."

"What?" Devaney's chair shoved back, and she was on her feet, moving away from them.

Blair stood, watching, before he was seated again. "How serious is he about this?"

"As serious as I have ever seen him." Benen shook his head. "I have no idea where he comes up with this, but he could be right. This is personal, what has happened. The man watching Devaney all this years? Likely hired by Bridget to keep her from getting here."

"But I didn't know where she was. So, again, why?"

"That's what our guys have picked up on, and are working through it." Benen looked past him at the doorway. "Barnabas is sending Brody and Brennen to Alberta. No offence to Will, but he thinks we need to do this. He has connections out there they'll be in contact with. He's not leaving anything undone this time. Devaney could have easily been killed. Or it could have been meant for you and you killed, Devaney being in the wrong position at the time. Right now, we're not sure which one was the target."

Blair sighed, his hands scrubbing down his face. "I wondered that, you know. I wondered if I was the target and Devaney got in the way. How do we proceed?"

"Leave it with us. The guys are out there now, Barnabas sent them out earlier today in the company jet. We're not talking to Will yet. Barnabas has said not to. Not until we can find out anything. He'll verify what we have and then pass it on."

An hour later, Blair stood, his eyes on Devaney as she slept, seeing the pain and stress on her face, and then turned and walked away, heading for the living room and the couch. He had some thinking to do, heavy at that from what he had been told, and some time to spend with God. He needed that.

Chapter 41

Three days later, Devaney took hesitant steps outside the building, fear rising within her. She didn't like that the violence had been brought there. Anyone could have been hurt, she decided, not seeing Cadee and Berneen watching her closely.

"It hurts, doesn't it?" Cadee's voice was quiet.

"It does. And we don't know which one of us was the target. That hurts even more." Devaney finally admitted her fear. "How did you two do this?"

"Prayer. Support from the team. Support from my brother for me. Support for her parents for Cadee." Berneen hugged Devaney. "It's different for you. You don't have family. Yes, you have your foster parents, but it's not the same." She studied the sky, seeing the grayness that had moved it. "How sure are you of them?"

Devaney shrugged. "I don't know. I think we're okay. I asked Benen to look into them. He said he would. I haven't heard that he found anything."

"Benen would tell you, but he would wait until he had proof." Cadee linked an arm with Devaney. "Now, what do we do with you? Doc says you can be outside but you have to take it easy."

Devaney shook her head. "I know what he said. I just can't not do anything." She looked up as well at the sky, a frown on her face before she rubbed at her forehead. "I hate this. I'm never sick."

They turned to head back into the building, finding seats in one of the sitting areas, Devaney's strength fading. Cadee and Berneen shared a glance before Cadee was off, back in short order with snacks and juice for them.

Devaney looked down at the bottle of juice she held, her thoughts muddled as she twisted at the cap. Her hand froze and her eyes slid closed. She had a sudden vision of doing the very same thing, only it wasn't juice that was in the bottle. She had thrown the bottle from her.

The two ladies with her watched as her face whitened and then Cadee reached for the bottle.

"Devaney? What did you remember?"

Devastated, she looked at the other women. "I remember doing this. Unscrewing a bottle cap. Only it wasn't juice. It wasn't water. It was poison. I could sense something off when I opened the cap. It didn't snap like it should have to be a new bottle. I threw it from me and ran as hard as I could."

"Where was this?" Cadee's arm was around her friend.

"In Winnipeg. He tracked me down in Winnipeg. Or she did. One of them did. Or was it someone else?" She looked up, a bleak look around her eyes. "How do I know who to trust? How do I keep Blair safe?"

Berneen watched her friend closely. "We'll work with this. Do you remember anything about it?"

"I'm trying but everything right now is so confusing. I'm getting glimpses of things, words, sentences, people. I just can't keep it all straight with the headaches I have."

"Then, this is what we do. We'll find you a notebook, and you'll right it all down. Does Blair have one?" Berneen's calm words reached through to Devaney.

"I'm not sure. I can look."

"Then, look we will." Cadee was on her feet, on a mission Benen would have said. "If he doesn't, I know we do."

Blair stood later that day, grubby from his work, needing to shower, but his concern was on Devaney, watching as she slept, stretched out on the couch, a soft blanket covering her. He smiled as he watched Anna's kitten curled up beside her, a tiny tongue grooming her paw. He knew how much Devaney loved her animals, and Anna must have shared. I don't know if you'll get your kitten back, Anna, but somehow I think you don't mind.

He finally moved back towards her, showered and in clean clothes, before he crouched down beside her, a hand on her face. Devaney stirred, her eyes blinking open and closed, even as a small smile emerged on her face.

"Have a good day, love?" Blair waited.

"I did. At least, I think I did. How about you? And what time is it?"

"Just after five." His hand kept her still. "Don't worry about getting up to get us dinner. I hear someone has been through with a meal for us."

"Brady. He dropped off lasagna. I didn't know he cooked."

"He does. He makes wonderful meals." He reached to help her sit up, sitting beside her. "What did you go and do?"

She shook her head. "Brady set the timer for us to heat the lasagna. It should be ready soon." She leaned against him. "Cadee and Berneen were here. I started a journal of everything. Berneen suggested it." She looked up, fear and stress and another emotion he couldn't quite read on her face. "I remembered something."

"What did you remember, my love?" He watched, and waited. "Devaney? What did you remember? It's scared you, hasn't it?"

She nodded, a grimace on her face as the headache hit her hard for a moment. "I remembered being in Winnipeg. I had a bottle of something, but I didn't drink it. I threw it away. I think it was poison." She looked back up at him as his arms tightened around her. "Who does this? Can't we find them and solve this?"

"We will, my love. It's getting to that point. Will wants to meet with us and the new detective in the morning. It's Saturday, I know, so I'm home. I told him it would depend on how you were."

"We need to, I guess, love. But not here. I won't have them here." She was becoming agitated, a frown on Blair's face as he studied her.

What is going on here, Lord? Something has triggered this.

Chapter 42

Mid-morning on the Saturday, Blair stepped back from the door, a frown on his face for a moment as Benen, Brody and Brandon entered. He sighed. I guess this means we don't meet with Will this morning. He reached to send a quick text off to Will to let him know they would be delayed.

"What's up, guys?" Blair pointed towards the kitchen. "Let me find Devaney."

"I'm right here." She peeked around Blair at the other three. "I don't like this. You've found something. Otherwise, you wouldn't be here."

"Sure, we would. We would come and see you." Benen grinned at her even as he accepted the mug of coffee and then pointed to the living room. "Can we sit in there? It will be more comfortable for Devaney."

Devaney sank to the couch, grateful that she could sit somewhere soft. She felt Blair's arm around her and then his words as he asked the men to pray. She knew they had found something, and whatever that something was, she would not like it.

Brody finally looked at the two, before he began to speak.

"As you know, Brandon and I headed west. That's beautiful country out there, guys."

"It is. I miss it at times, but Ontario does grow on you. Especially this part." Blair watched his

——

183

friends intently, seeing the discomfort they were showing. "So, tell us. What did you find?"

The three men shared a look before Brody spoke up.

"We have talked with your foster parents. They had no idea what was going on. They wished you had talked to them, Devaney, but understand why you didn't. They were threatened as well, weren't they?" Brody gave a grim smile as she finally gave a small nod. "That's what we had thought. Now, as to what happened out there. We have talked with friends of yours, with your teachers from high school, your college professors. All claim not to have known what was going on, that you were imagining all this. That you had never really planned to marry Blair, but were simply leading him along and had planned to disappear all along."

Devaney stared at him, her mouth snapping closed. "Who said that? That's a lie."

"We know know it is. We have talked to many people who tell us that you and Blair were in love, that they knew you would marry, but they were saddened and shocked when you didn't and simply disappeared. You are loved and missed greatly, Devaney."

Brandon took over. "We've stopped in different towns, where we thought you may have been. In the small towns, you were remembered. The ones we talked to were helpful. They have given impressions and descriptions of the man and woman who watched you."

"People saw them? I didn't imagine them?"

"No, you didn't imagine them. There are occasions where these people have admitted to helping you escape, to finding ways to direct these two away from you, and helping you to escape." He paused for a moment, to gather his thoughts and his emotions. "I can't imagine living like you did. Running for your life at times. Not trusting that God was even there." He smiled as her eyes slid closed and a tear trickled down her face. "He was there, all along, protecting you, taking care of you, providing for you."

She nodded, her eyes closed as she tried to control her emotions, finally just turning into Blair's shoulder as he held her, his chin on her head.

"What else, guys?" Blair finally asked the question Devaney was unable to frame.

"We have spoken with the couple that you named. They are under arrest in Toronto. We can't say why but they did mean you two harm. Their words were along the line of you two deserved everything that happened to you. Investigators are tracking their steps and also their connection to Bridget and Jerry. There seems to be a connection but they haven't given us that information. They will be in touch with Will."

"So, I don't understand. What else did you find out?" Devaney sighed. "And we still have to meet with Will."

"He said this afternoon is fine. I got a text back from him." Blair's thoughts were puzzled. "I still don't see how they fit in."

Devaney's eyes slid closed. "I know why. When I was ten, Jerry was in the foster home I was at for a couple of hours. I think you'll find that out somehow and that he is connected to Bridget. I sort of remember comments that aren't clear, about a female cousin." She looked up at the men. "If I had remembered sooner, would this have not happened?"

Benen shook his head. "It would have. They seem determined to harm you in some way. We're taking steps to keep you two as safe as we can, but we can't be with you all the time." He looked over at Blair. "I heard you did some remembering yesterday."

"I did, thanks to your wife and Berneen." She pointed to the coffee table. "It's there. Everything I can remember and everything I didn't know I could. We looked through it last night. Take it with you. If you need to, talk to Will. I would rather he didn't have it yet."

"That we can do." Benen reached for it, flipping through it quickly, amazed at what she had been able to remember. "God is bringing up what you've buried."

"He is. Sometimes I wish He wouldn't."

Chapter 43

Will studied the young couple as he directed them to an office, motioning for Dallas to come with them. The young detective had never met them but felt he knew them. He shook his head at the way Bridget had worked, knowing she was not what she had claimed to be. It was a shame, he thought. Devaney being shot may well have been avoided, if we could have found these people in time. And find them, he would. Dallas had a good idea that Blair's friends were working on something. He had been contacted by the Toronto investigators and had multiple contacts from police agencies across the country, all with information on what Devaney had faced and how worried they were about her.

Devaney sat, her hand reaching for Blair's, as both of them watched Will closely, before turning their attention to Dallas. Will introduced him and then sat, his thoughts becoming clearer.

"Devaney. Blair. We are finally making progress. I can't apologize enough for what you two went through."

"We know, Will. We know. We get that she was playing you." Blair paused, his eyes thoughtful. "Who else did she do this to?"

"No one that we can see. She was planted here, Blair, that much we know. They were watching Devaney move your way and were just waiting for you two to connect. We think she's the one who hired the man who ran you off the road." Dallas spoke, his voice full of confidence that he had the truth finally for them. He stared down at the folder on the table. "I have been out west, spoken with numerous people out there." He frowned for a moment. "There have been both positive and negative, though."

"About what we thought." Devaney spoke, her eyes steady on Dallas. "You'll find people will say I was a fake, that Blair was a fake, that we never planned to marry, it was all a hoax. That we were planning to rip people off. That Blair leaving was a sign of guilt. How am I doing?"

Dallas stared at her, then shook his head, smiling at her. "Just about right, I'd say."

"And then you'll have people who support us. If you look closely at the two groups, you'll find them divided as to who they support and who has gotten to them. Those that know us know the truth." Blair nodded towards the folder. "What else do you have for us? Devaney's been up for too long and needs to be sleeping."

Dallas nodded, understanding what Blair was not saying. "We have spoken with the police in Toronto about that couple. They have been arrested. Charges will be pending against them here as we have evidence they hired the gunmen. There were two, you understand. We working on determining just which one of you it was."

"It was likely both of us. We kept them from their plans, whatever they were. We needed to die."

Devaney's head went down on Blair as she had difficulty keeping her eyes open. "What else?"

"We are talking to police agencies across the country, following your trail, Devaney. Do you realize how close you were at times to dying?" Will had been shocked, to say the least, when he found that out.

"I do now. I have the scars from some of those attempts. And I threw away a bottle likely containing poison in Winnipeg." She stood, her mouth open to speak, and then walked away, her steps faltering as her hand went to her head.

"Call me when you can, Dallas. Will." Blair walked away, stopping to sweep Devaney into his arms, before he headed for his vehicle, Branigan and Brady waiting for him. They had not let them come on their own.

Blair stared down at Devaney as he cradled her close to him, his thoughts muddled, but his heart praying before he looked up, his eyes on Brady who was driving.

"They don't know much more than what you've found out. Find these people, please? She can't take much more."

"No, she can't. And neither can you. It may mean putting you two away somewhere." Branigan twisted enough in his seat to watch them.

"We won't go. I know Devaney. She'll be out there searching for them. She's had enough. And frankly, so have I."

"We'll find them. I spoke with Burnie. He has some new thoughts he's working through with Benen. Those two are a scary team, you know."

Blair laughed. "They are. That they are." He stepped down from the truck, reaching for his lady, carrying her through to their apartment, not seeing the compassionate eyes on them, the eyes that sought each other and then the men gathered in the boardroom, Devaney's notes in front of them, determination to solve that mystery surrounding their friends that day, if at all possible. Buckley led off in prayer and then Barnabas spoke words of encouragement to them all.

Chapter 44

Pacing the boardroom the next afternoon, Devaney wrapped her arms around herself. She didn't like that they were working on Sunday. She sighed to herself as she remembered church that morning.

Blair had simply walked her in, her hand in his, and seated her near the back of the church. Berneen and Baird had sat on one side of them, Benen and Cadee on the other. She saw the speculative looks she was given and then the nods as her hand had raised to brush hair from her face, and they saw her rings. Blair's arm around her had tightened as he sensed her discomfort.

He had not let her stay long after the service, simply sweeping her away, leaving comments and questions in the air, ones that his friends had answered. Neither knew the support they had garnered from their church family, with offers to help flying at the men.

Blair watched as she paced, knowing she needed to do this, but also knowing it was wearing her down. How, Lord, do we stop this? How do we end this? What piece of the puzzle do we not have or don't know we have that would end this? Please, dear Lord, I need this over for my lady.

Breck paused beside Blair, his eyes on his friend.

"Blair, how are you?"

Blair shrugged. "I am no longer sure, Breck. I need this over for her and I just don't know where to turn to find that missing piece. It's like a big jigsaw puzzle we are putting together and the key piece we need is not there."

Devaney had paused as she listened to him before she turned, her eyes searching.

"Devaney?" Barnabas stood beside her. "What are you looking for? What do you need?"

"I need to visualize everything. Is there a large map of Canada we can put up on the wall? One that I can mark up?"

Bradon had looked up at her words and was away and then back with a large map that was attached to the wall, handing her a marker.

"I can't write on this. It's too nice."

"Write on it, Devaney. I can always get another one if I need to. Right now, you need this. Tell us what you want to write. We'll do it for you." He gently shoved her into a chair, taking back the marker.

An hour later, she walked past the map, her finger tracing her steps across the country, her face pale at how far she had travelled on her own for so many months and years. "Did I really do this?"

"You did. Fear drove you as did your love for Blair." Buckley grinned at her as she heard the murmurs of agreement from the men. "You tried to bury that, tried to hide it, deny it, but it's the catalyst that forced you to keep moving. You wanted him safe and you knew you had to find him."

"You're right." She paused, turning to find Blair. "He's right, Blair. I denied it, but he's right."

"I know you are, love." Blair's smile helped her to control her emotions, seeing his love and belief in her shining through. "Now, what do we do about that?" He pointed at the map.

Burnie walked up to him, his finger tracing her route. "There's something here, Devaney, something that you saw or heard or noticed that carried with you from Alberta. I would say that when you were attacked, that's when one of them was around you and decided you needed to pay for whatever it was."

"I think you're right." She studied the map and then him, before turning finding all eyes on her. "You all have a different occupation, right?" At their nods, she continued. "And different organizations you volunteer for?" Again there were nods. "So, how be if you look at this, look at what I've written, what Brandon and Brody discovered, and then note what you observe from your point of view. Not mine. Not theirs. Pull it apart as much as you can and then we'll fit it back together. Does that work?"

Brennen spoke up. "That's what we'll do, Devaney. I think you have just given us what we need to do. We will solve this, I promise you that. We'll solve this and then you can get on with your life."

She nodded, seeing Anna approaching her. "Anna?"

"Come with me for a bit, Devaney. Let the men work. If they have questions, they'll just write them down and then ask you. I think doing this will let us finally work it all out for you." She led Devaney from the room and to her apartment. "Sit, dear. I need to prepare some food for the men. You need to rest." She set a cup of tea in front of her before she sat. "What can I do just for you?"

"For me? You're doing so much all ready. What more can you do?"

Anna shook her head at the questioning look she was given. "Devaney. You are hurting in more ways than just physical. You need to heal. Doc can help you heal physically. But in other ways, you need to heal. I know you've renewed your faith. I can see that. Just reach out for that garment's hem, dear. He is waiting for you to do just that." Anna's arms were around Devaney as the younger woman wept, tears of healing spilling up and out, tears she could not control and made no effort to.

Chapter 45

Looking for her later, Blair looked up as the door to the boardroom opened and the four ladies entered, trays in their hand. Doc followed with the large coffee urn that he set on a table and plugged in, quiet words to Cadee as she arranged mugs and creamer and sugar around it. A large teapot was added.

Barnabas rose, heading for Anna, taking her tray from her with a quiet word of thanks. He looked around, knowing they had made a lot of progress on their own. They now needed to combine their thoughts, ideas, and findings, but first they would take a break.

"Doc, lead us in prayer for the food, please." Doc nodded at Barnabas' words.

An hour later, Barnabas once more stood watching his men, the ladies with them, turning to watch Doc and Anna, and then finding Blair and Devaney. He could see the fatigue in them and wanted this over for them. How, Lord, how do we do this?

The men shared what they had each discovered or thought of, each one different. Doc had volunteered to be the scribe, writing everything down on paper taped to the wall. He drew arrows, lines, crossed out words, and added ideas and thoughts before he moved to a clean page and began to write facts called out from each man.

Blair watched, a growing conviction in his heart that they were on the right track. Devaney was tired, having trouble concentrating, before her head went down on her folded arms on the table and she slept, Blair's arm around her. Doc shook his head.

"She needs to be in bed, Blair. Not here."

"She won't leave, Doc. Not even if it destroys her health. She's mad, she tired, she's had enough. She wants this over. And frankly, so do I. We can't go on with our lives with this hanging over our heads."

"We know you can't. Will and Dallas are working as hard as they can. So are our guys." Doc studied the wall and the writing on the papers. "I would say they have made a good start. Someone will need to get this to Will or Dallas."

"Not yet. There's something missing." Blair looked down as Devaney mentioned a name, her eyes cracking open just a fraction of an inch. "Devaney? You're sure?"

"I am. Search and prove me right or wrong." Devaney slept again, her trust in Blair that he would do just that.

Benen frowned at the name. "They live here, don't they? How did she connect them?"

"That's what we'll have to look into. I would suspect somehow with Bridget." Blair sat back, deep in thought, looking up as Brendon spoke.

"She's right. That's our connection. They were originally from your hometown, Blair. And they are related to Bridget. And to Jerry."

Benen reached for the paperwork Brendon had printed. "That's how it is, then. Who gets to talk to Will?"

"I guess I do." Brendon sighed. "I can tomorrow. Let's condense this, finish off for the day, and let Blair and Devaney head home."

Will stared at Brendon the next day, his hand stopped in midair as he reached for the sheaf of papers Brendon was thrusting at him.

"You did what?"

"We worked through all this. Devaney asked us to look at it from each of our perspectives from work and volunteering. She was right to do that. We all saw something different that made a whole lot of sense." He thrust the paperwork into Will's hands. "This is the condensed version of it." He paused, biting at his lip. "She also gave us another name. They're related to both Bridget and Jerry."

"So she was right, wasn't she? I could use her on the force."

"I doubt that would ever happen. I have no idea what she wants to do. She hasn't had a chance to live freely in years. So I don't expect her to rush into anything."

Will shook his head. "I agree with you." He looked down at the paperwork. "I know you fellows are good. You'll have given us any links and websites that we need. All the information we can use to find these people. And we will find them. I can't tell you much, but Dallas is forging ahead on this." He sighed. "I wish he had been on it from the beginning. We not likely would be having this conversation."

Brendon shook his head. "I think we would have been having some form of it. We needed Devaney to start remembering, and to protect herself, she buried it very deep."

"That she did. If any of you come up with anything else, call me or Dallas."

"We'll do that." Brendon walked away, leaving Will staring after him before he searched for Dallas.

"Dallas? Barnabas' guys were busy. They've sent this for you?"

Dallas turned from the copier, papers in his hand, as he stared at the papers in Will's hands. "What have they done?"

Will explained what Brendon had shared before Dallas took the paperwork, quickly flipping through it.

"This is good. It will help. But that's not all?" He eyed his chief closely.

"No, it's not." Will sighed, given the name of the couple and their likely relationship to Bridget and Jerry.

"That's what we had suspicions of. I'll prove it." Dallas walked away, knowing his work had increased, but he was determined to solve the problem or mystery or whatever you wanted to call it, he thought.

Chapter 46

Standing near the lake the next morning, Devaney shivered, looking around her. She could feel the evil and suddenly turned and ran, heading for the building, sliding to a stop as a man appeared in her pathway. She turned and ran for the woods, finding a path to follow, praying it led her to safety. Hearing the heavy footsteps and cursing and yells behind her spurred her feet to a faster pace. She saw the building in front of her and ran harder, her breath coming in gasps as her chest heaved with the exertion.

Sliding to a stop just inside the doors, Devaney spun, her eyes searching for the man after her, hearing the security guard approaching her and then the man urging her away from the doors and windows. He followed her up to the apartment, admonishing her to lock the doors after her, and if she needed to go anywhere, to call him.

The man looked for Barnabas or Breck, letting them know how he had found Devaney. Grim looks covered their faces and were shared. The man or woman after Devaney was getting desperate, willing even to be on the property to try and kidnap her.

Blair's face paled as he listened to Breck that evening, before he almost ran for his wife, his shoes hitting the boot tray, the door locked behind him, as he searched, finding her in his office, asleep in his favourite chair there. He stood and watched, seeing new lines of stress on her face, the paleness of it, and the pain etched there.

He grew angry, and determined. This would end and end now, he thought. But how? He moved away to change from his work clothes, coming back to scoop Devaney into his arms and sit, cradling her close to him. He gave a smile as he saw Anna's kitten sneaking through the room, to pounce up on the chair arm before she curled up on Devaney.

Devaney roused, for a moment fearful, then hearing Blair praying for them. She raised her head, studying him.

"Blair?" She was puzzled, confused as to time. Her head was hurting more today than it had and that scared her.

"Devaney? Are you okay? Breck told me what happened."

Her head went back down on his shoulder, even as her hands clenched together, her face pale and drawn. "I don't feel good, Blair. My head is really hurting."

He stared at her, then was on his feet, carrying her towards Doc's, knowing he was home. Doc took one look at her and pointed back out the door, heading for the infirmary.

Blair stood and watched as Doc made his examination, then stood back.

"Doc?"

"We need to repeat the imaging, Blair, and now. I'm sending her in by ambulance, asking that a CT scan be run stat. I know she ran for her life today.

Whether that has triggered something or not, I don't know. We need to find out."

Blair nodded, watching as the paramedics arrived and then headed out with Devaney, following by Blair, who refused to let her out of his sight. He didn't see the men who had gathered to watch, Cadee and Berneen heading for a vehicle to follow.

"Doc?" Barnabas spoke from bedside him.

"She's hurting, Barnabas. Just a precaution. But her headaches should be easing." He paused. "Do you know if she's been taking her pain medication?"

"I'm not sure." His phone was out, a quick text sent to Blair. "He says she has but I wonder. Doc, come with me. Blair's told me to go in and find it and then bring it with me."

Doc looked at the bottle. "It says what was prescribed." Popping open the top, he dumped some out into his hand. "No, this is wrong. These are not them. Someone's gotten to them."

Barnabas' face grew stern. "So either it was dispensed wrong, or someone has been in here."

"I would suspect someone has been in here. And through the balcony."

Barnabas was across the room and scanning the door. "You're right. Someone has jimmied it by the looks of it. They wouldn't have caught it as they not likely have had the doors open."

Doc was out the door, Barnabas on his heels, a quick word to Breck, who stood, stunned, his eyes following them before he turned and ran for the security desk, questions flying from him.

Blair watched as Doc handed the medication bottle to the treating physician, their words too quiet to hear, before Doc waled towards him.

"Doc?"

"She wasn't taking the right medication, Blair. We have to test to see what it is but it was not the pain medication prescribed for her." He paused, not sure how to continue. "Someone got in through your balcony doors."

Blair sighed, his head going back as his eyes closed, his hands jammed into his jacket pockets. "She was right after all."

"What do you mean?" Doc looked up as Will and Dallas stopped beside Blair.

"She said she thought someone had been in the apartment but we couldn't see any evidence of it. She thought she was wrong."

"She wasn't, Blair." He spun as Will spoke, not having heard him come towards him. "She has instincts you don't see often."

"I know she does. She always has had." He watched as she slept, the pain easing from her face. "How do we find these monsters? We can't go on like this. It will kill her."

Will nodded, his eyes on Dallas, who was lost in thought before he excused himself and walked away, his phone out to make a call. "We know it's hard. We know she was approached today." He sighed, not knowing how to respond fully.

Chapter 47

Blair paced the apartment the next night, knowing that Devaney had already retired and was asleep. This is so hard, he thought. At least her pain is better, and those pills didn't harm her, not that we know of. He spun, an idea running through his mind. Who could he talk to, he wondered?

His phone out, his finger scrolled through his contacts, finding one from years ago. He frowned. No, he thought, it couldn't be, could it? Blair sighed, knowing he had just added another name to the list, and sent a text off with it to both Will and Dallas.

Dallas' voice on the other end of the line startled him when he answered the call.

"Blair? How sure are you?"

"I'm not, but he's the only one who I've really kept in contact with over the years. Could it be him?"

"It could. His is one name that came up. Did you know he's related to that couple?"

"He is? And no, I didn't."

"He's a nephew of the wife. They have tried to say they have had no contact with one another but phone records show otherwise. We have tracked his records. He has been in the cities and towns where your wife was attacked."

—

Blair sank down to the floor, his head against the wall, his eyes sliding shut. "I've been the one, then."

"The one who?"

"The one driving this."

"No, I don't think you are. We're finding motives that aren't totally connected to either one of you, but there are motives connected to you both."

"Okay, then. How do we do this? What do we do?"

"You two do nothing. You go to work. Devaney works on healing. We will want you to be seen out and about. Take her out for a meal, a walk, shopping. As much as she can handle. Go about your daily walk. Does she work?"

Blair's eyes slid closed again. "No, she doesn't. She won't have to. I'm not sure if you are aware, but as we guys marry, an income is settled on the wives, so they don't have to work, or if they work, it's the same arrangement as us. Someone hires them, but the Foundation pays their wages."

"I see. So there is no motive there." Dallas' voice faded away for a moment, then came back stronger. Blair could hear papers rustling in the background.

"Dallas? You have a thought?"

"I did, but if her income comes from there, and not an inheritance or trust, then there's no motive that way."

"She has no inheritance or trust. We've looked into that."

"Okay." Dallas was silent for a moment. "I have an idea I need to think through. If you will be home tomorrow, I would like to stop by."

"Tomorrow night would work."

"Then, I'll see you tomorrow night. Get some rest, Blair. You need it."

"Thank you and you too."

Devaney turned from the doorway, knowing Blair had not heard her. She had listened to his side of the conversation, recognizing the name he had spoken, and knowing that the man named had not been a true friend of his. She had wanted to tell him but didn't know how.

The next night, Blair stood back from the door, watching as Dallas entered, greeting him and seeing him greet Devaney, a frown on his face. Something had changed in the last twenty four hours and that concerned him.

Blair and Devaney listened as Dallas spoke, their eyes meeting every once in a while.

"And how close are you to an arrest?" Blair was pushing, and they all knew it.

"Within the next forty-eight hours I suspect. We have just about all the evidence on everyone, including the name you gave me." He looked up, as Devaney made a sound. "Devaney?"

"It was him, all along. It was him. He's the one who threatened Branigan in Regina. He's the one who has been chasing me. He's been using Bridget and Jerry to do his work, but he's behind it. He's related to that couple and using them too."

Dallas shook his head. "How did you just do that?"

"Do what?" Devaney looked at him, before she shared a look with Blair

"Come to that conclusion so quick. It's taken us a lot of work and time."

"You have to have the evidence. I know them. That's how I did this." She burrowed against Blair, just needing to be held.

Blair nodded. "She does know them. She picks up on people in a way few I have seen can do."

"I can see that. We need her on the force."

Blair laughed at that even as he felt Devaney's head shaking. "She won't. I don't know what she wants to do, but policing is not it."

"No, not that. I don't know what I want to do. I have had so many jobs, all low paying, that I want to take some time. I've had to take them to survive. That's no way to live." She looked up as Blair shook his head. "Blair?"

"We need to talk, love, but you don't have to work. I explained to Dallas, but you and I need to talk. With the Foundation, you know it pays our wages, the guys?" When she nodded, he continued. "It is set up that when the guys marry, the Foundation pays their wives a wage. I'll let Barnabas explain it in detail to you as well as the amount you will receive, but you don't have to work. You have an income coming to you. You can work or you can volunteer or even go back to school to train in something new. It is your choice."

She stared at him, dumbfounded. "This is for real?"

"It is, love. It's how Barnabas and his father wanted it."

"Well, I don't know what to say. I didn't know that. It's not common knowledge?"

Blair shook his head. "No, it's not. It's confidential among us."

"Okay, so that's not why they were after me." She paused, a look of horror almost crossing her face. "Is it about Barnabas? Nothing started until you had been approached about working here."

Dallas and Blair shared a look, Dallas shaking his head at the new thought.

"We considered that, love, but we don't see that. No one knew Barnabas had approached me. He did it through a lawyer that knows the Foundation. We met privately. I hadn't made my decision until about two days before graduation."

She shrugged. "I know. It was just an idea, but who's to say that wasn't part of it?"

Chapter 48

A week later, her hand tight in Blair's, Devaney walked the downtown of her new city, or town or village, she wasn't quite sure what to call it. She liked it. A small place, she thought, where you can know your neighbours.

Blair watched the flickering emotions cover her face, seeing the healing. He knew the headaches had greatly improved since they found the medication switch and had become much less frequent. He could see her heart healing as well, knowing from her prayers she had found her way back to God. He thanked the Lord for that, for the healing she had undergone.

"So, where is this store I just had to see?" She looked up at him, a quick grin on her face.

"Right here." He paused to open the door, waiting for her to walk through before following her. He nodded at Sam, the owner as he moved to the counter.

"Blair? This is a jewelry store."

"I know it is. I know you've worn my ring for years and now have a matching band. But I want to find something special for you."

She shook her head. "You don't have to. It's not necessary."

"But it is. I've missed out on years of bringing you jewelry. I plan to rectify that."

Devaney stared at him, recognizing what he was saying, without him having to put it into words, and nodded. She looked down at the simple engraved gold bracelet that he fastened on her wrist before he kissed her cheek.

They wandered the town, knowing they were being followed and watched. They had seen the man Blair had named and knew he was not alone. At this point, neither cared about that. They were ready to confront him and had given Dallas an ultimatum, which he had vigorously talked them out of. He needed them to let the police do their work.

Walking away from him, they had exchanged a glance, knowing that they would only allow so much time and then would put their plan into action. They had talked to no one, not even the men from the Foundation, knowing it would put them at risk.

Branigan and Bradon had followed the two, not being seen but watching the watchers as Bradon had half-laughing called them. They all knew the couple were ready to break loose and confront their enemies and wanted to be ready to help them.

Bradon pointed to Blair. "He's ready to run."

"I know he is. There he goes. Come on, Bradon. We need to keep him in sight." Branigan ran down the sidewalk, Bradon behind him, dodging pedestrians and benches and planter boxes. He slid to a halt. "Where did they go?"

"They've disappeared. I don't like this." He spun in a circle. "I think they were taken."

"I think you're right." Branigan's hand on Bradon pulled him in the direction they had last see the couple.

"They're not here. They can't have disappeared this quickly." Bradon's phone was out and he was quickly speaking with Barnabas. Sticking it away, he turned once more in a circle. "Barnabas is finding the guys and will be in. Where do we look for them?"

Barnabas stood and watched his friends before he moved forward. "No sign of them?"

"No. And no sign of the men we saw watching them. They were gone so quickly. I don't think this was their plan."

"No, I don't think it was. I spoke with both Will and Dallas. They're searching as well. Dallas said he was ready to make arrests and did I know how this complicated the situation?"

The two men with him gave grim smiles.

"We know that. And I am sure that Blair and Devaney didn't plan this. I know they were planning something in the next few days. But not today. That I know. Blair just wanted a day out with Devaney. He said they needed that." Bradon stood, his eyes searching.

"They did. It was what whoever it was watching for." Branigan agreed.

Chapter 49

Devaney's hand tight in his, Blair closely watched the two men who held weapons on them, his heart falling. This wasn't supposed to happen, not today. Today had been about getting Devaney out and about, falling more in love with her. Not about facing men with weapons. He felt her hand tighten on his. Yes, he thought, he knew these men. Lord, we need Your help to get out of this.

They walked forward as directed, entering the door that led to a second floor, turning as directed to sit in the chairs set just right for them. Devaney gave a small whimper as her hands were tied, the weapon against Blair's head keeping him from moving as his hands were tied as well.

Time passed as they waited. They watched the sun's rays grow longer and darkness appear before a light was turned on. Heavy drapes were pulled across the windows, leaving the night blocked from their sight.

Their gazes raised to the door as they heard it open and then glanced at one another. They had been right after all. Bridget and Jerry were connected to the Watsons. The four stood in front of them.

Devaney stared at them, then looked around them. "Where is he?"

"Where's who? There's no one else." Bridget sneered at her.

"But there is. Tony Watson. Where is he? You don't have the smarts, none of you, to have planned and carried out this." Devaney was defiant, knowing she had to draw them out in order to end it.

"What are you talking about? Of course, we've planned this." Jerry was arrogant, sure of his facts, he thought.

Blair shook his head. "No, not at all. I know you all. You're just doing what Tony has told you to."

They began to argue among themselves, drawing away and to another room. Devaney had worked at her bonds, finding them loosening. She shrugged them off, rising quietly and working on Blair's, finding his hand and drawing him away and out the door, moving swiftly to the back of the building and down. She opened the door, Blair's hand on her, and then ran from the building, heading for the police department and safety.

Dallas stared at her before he was on the move, heading for the building, officers with him, Will bringing them back to safety. He just shook his head at their words.

Devaney paced, Blair keeping step with her, until Dallas approached them. Hope sprang on their faces.

"We have them. We're still look for Tony."

"Of course, you do. He's a coward and will hide. That's a given." Devaney spun and walked away, Blair shrugging as he followed her.

"Devaney? It's not his fault."

"I know it's not. I just want this over. Where is God today. Blair?"

"He's here, love. He got us away from them."

She hugged him tight. "Take me home, please? Just take me home."

"I will. Except we need to walk to where my truck is. And it's dark."

Will stood there. "Come on, you two. I'll drive you home. Blair, let me have your keys. I'll have an officer follow me with it."

Will hit the brakes of his car as he saw the roadblock ahead of him, reaching for his radio, confirming there was nothing that should be there.

"Stay put you two. I need to look into this." He was from his car, the officer out of Blair's truck as they moved towards the road block, both men going down as they were shot at. Blair reached for the radio, frantically calling in that they needed help. He could hear the sirens in the distance before the door beside him was pulled open and he was yanked for the seat, hearing Devaney's small scream as she was pulled out as well.

They were shoved forward past Will and the officer, seeing movement from them, before they were roughly pushed down an embankment and up the other side, made to walk through debris until they reached a cabin. The door was pulled open roughly and they were propelled inside, barely keeping to their feet. They heard the door slammed shut and a lock snapped loudly shut.

Their eyes on one another, Blair drew Devaney to him, his arms tight around her, his heart raising in a prayer for safety and rescue.

"What was that?" Devaney's voice was low and shaky.

"I think that was Tony. He knew we were free. Somehow, I think there's a leak on the force. I pray not, but it's too obvious someone knows what we're doing."

"Someone who Grace has gotten to. Or maybe Tony." Devaney blew out a breath. "Where does this end?" She walked away from Blair before spinning and moving back. "Will? And that officer?"

"They were alive. I just don't know how hurt they were." Blair paced the cabin. "I know this place. It's on the Foundation property."

"Can you get us out of here?"

"I'm certainly going to try." He reached for the windows, shoving at them. "They've blocked them. They planned this. They let us get away tonight."

"That's what I wondered. It was too easy. Do they know they were set up?"

"Not likely." Blair stood, a hand on the door, searching the room, his eyes raising to the roof. "This cabin. It's the one with the leak. That means the roof is compromised."

He searched for a chair, dragging it over to a corner of the room, and standing on it. "We did some preliminary work here, just to mitigate the damage."

"My, my. What big words you're using?" Devaney grinned up at him for a moment, before she sobered. "Can we get out?"

"We'll make an effort. Just listen for anyone coming."

Devaney was by the door, her ear to it, her eyes on Blair as he worked away, finally seeing moon light through the ceiling, and was back at his side as he motioned her. His hands pulled her up beside him and then guided her to the roof, following quickly as he heard her drop down.

She stared at him. "Did we really just do that?"

"We did. Now, come on. Let's get you back to the building." His hand reached for hers as he ran from the clearing towards a path he knew would lead them to that very place.

Branigan stared at them as they entered through a back door, before he was with them, his hands motioning them towards an empty suite. Inside, he locked the door and then just stood and stared at them.

"Will said you had been taken captive again."

Blair gave a grim smile. "We were. They locked us into the white cabin."

"The one with the roof." Branigan was quick to understand. "Stay here. I'll get to Berneen or Cadee and get some clean clothes for you. We'll keep it quiet that you're here." He reached to hug them both, prayers of praise rising from him.

Chapter 50

Will stared at Doc as he buttoned his shirt back up, finished with his assessment at Emergency. His chest hurt, but his vest had done its work, keeping him alive. The patrol officer had been hit in the arm but survived, and he was thankful God had spared their lives.

"What do you mean, Doc?"

Doc shook his head, pointing at the door. "I said, they're fine. We have them somewhere safe."

Will breathed a sigh of relief. "I won't ask, because I know you won't tell me. They're okay? They're not hurt?"

"Physically, no. I can't answer for any other way. That's we'll have to look after once this is over."

"I know. Tell them to stay hidden. We're moving in on the last one but until we have him, they're not safe."

Doc nodded. "I know they're not. This was not what they planned. At least not today."

"I know. They did plan to put themselves out there. We're trying to prevent that. Today, that took everyone by surprise." Will paced the small area before he turned to study Doc. "Doc?"

Doc just shook his head. "Find them, Will. And soon. If you don't, then these two will be back out there." He paused, a frown on his face. "It just seems so bizarre. The way they could just walk out of there."

"That's what we think. The ones we have in custody aren't talking, but you know how I think. We've been friends for too many years, worked too many times together."

"And now you need to go. Go home, Will. Let your deputy chief take over for tonight. Those are medical orders."

Will sighed. "I knew you would say that. No talking you out of it?"

Doc grinned. "No. Your wife is waiting for you."

Doc turned from the door in the apartment late that night, his eyes on Blair, assessing his young friend before he nodded and headed for the kitchen. He needed a cup of coffee and he knew Blair would have some on. It had been a busy night, made worse by the shooting of the two officers. He thanked God they were safe, could go home to the families.

Blair slid into a chair, his head turning for a moment as he listened for Devaney, knowing it would be a night he would have little sleep. She would be up and down. That was a given, knowing what she had gone through in the past. The dreams and nightmares would drive their time that time.

"Doc? Will and the officer?"

"They're fine. Will's vest protected him. The officer was hit in the arm but is okay."

Blair's eyes shut. Thank you, Lord. "That scared Devaney. She thought they were dead when we were forced past them."

"I am sure she did. How is she?"

Blair shrugged. "She's sleeping but it will be a night of broken sleep for us both. It is what happens when the dreams and nightmares take over." He held up a hand as Doc went to speak. "She won't take anything. I've already tried that route. She is adamant she won't."

"No, I didn't think she would. What can we do for her?"

"I'm not sure what we can do. When it gets too bad, then I just hold her and pray."

"That's all you can do for now." Doc sipped at his coffee. "Will thinks they'll be able to arrest the man in the next day or so. They're closing in on his address."

"It can't be soon enough, but somehow I don't think they'll take him without a fight or without him finding us. He'll know we'd come back here."

"And the past has proven that they can get in and get to whoever it is they want." Doc was frustrated, knowing how hard it would be. "Has Barnabas been around?"

"No. We're trying to keep it quiet where we are. Branigan has been. He's relaying anything between us."

"That's good." Doc rose. "Call me if you need me, and I mean that, Blair. Anna's quite taken with your lady."

"Thanks, Doc. She needs Anna, whether she'll admit it or not. She's never had someone like that just for her. Even with our foster mother, she was busy with her own kids and whoever it was that came through from the system."

"Anna understands that. She's willing to be the mother Devaney needs. Her heart just expands to take another one in."

Blair laughed. "That's exactly what she does."

Locking the door after Doc, and turning out some lights, Blair sighed. This was not how he had planned their day, not one bit. He walked through the small suite, heading for the bedroom, turning out lights as he went. The mugs in the kitchen could wait until morning and then he detoured back to set the coffee for the morning and rinse out their mugs, setting them to dry. Blair stood, his hands resting on the countertop, his head hanging down. This needs to end, Lord, but how do we do just that?

Chapter 51

Devaney paced the next morning, her arms folded around herself, her eyes avoiding Blair, knowing he wanted to talk with her. He sighed, finally just reaching to stop her and sweep her into a tight hug.

"Blair? Who was here last night? I thought I heard voices."

"It was Doc. Just came to check on us. He said Will and the officer are fine." He felt her relax at his words. "You were worried, weren't you?"

"I was. Enough people have been hurt by this monster. How do we stop him?"

"We don't. Will was adamant on that. We leave it to him and his department." He leaned back to study her. "We need to talk, but first we need to spend time in prayer."

She sighed, shoving away from him. "We do. This time, I am afraid. Really afraid. Before this, I was just mad. This monster could and would kill anyone who gets in his way."

"He will. That's why we leave it with Will and his people." He drew her down on the couch, his arm around her.

Later that morning, he looked out the peephole, then opened the door for Branigan.

"Branigan, you have word?"

Branigan nodded. "They found him. Where's Devaney?"

"Right here." Her arm went around Blair's waist. "What did you say?"

"They found him, Devaney. We think it's over"

"What did he have to say?"

Branigan was silent, his eyes on the floor, not wanting to be the one to tell them what had happened.

"Branigan?" Blair's voice brought his head up. "He's dead?"

"He is. He tried to kill an officer. They had no choice."

"No, they wouldn't. But it doesn't answer the question of why." Devaney leaned harder against Blair.

"No, but it might. Dallas got word to us that there are many notebooks filled with information. They have to work through it. But until they're sure he was working on his own, they want you two to stay here in the building. You can go back to your own home."

They spoke for a bit longer and then Branigan slipped away, leaving Blair and Devaney to stare at one another. They finally walked away from the suite, heading for their own place. Once there, Devaney stood for a moment and then walked through to the office, heading for Blair's computer.

"What are you thinking?" He perched on the side of the desk.

"That he' married and now his wife will be coming after us." She looked up at him, a bleak look around her eyes. "We're here but we're still not safe. And we are putting everyone else at risk."

Blair nodded. "I know we are, but they will have it no other way, you know that. Dallas is to report back to us later tonight." He nodded at the computer. "I am sure they will be looking for his wife."

She sat back, her eyes on him, before she looked at the computer monitor. "I'm sure they will, but there is still something about all this. I can't put my finger on it."

"Neither can I. Come on, my love. Let's find some food and then you need to sleep. Your eyes are tired."

She sighed. "I am tired. I think I'll just go to bed. Call me when Dallas calls."

He was on his feet hours later, running for the bedroom, hearing Devaney's whimpers and knowing she would be screaming next. His arms around her, he rocked her back and forth, listening to her sobs and then the words she was saying. His heart broke for his lady, knowing she had been in so much danger over the years, and he hadn't been there for him.

He rose finally, watching her as she slept, determination in his mind. He would search for the one person who could end all this, putting his own life on the line to find her. And it was a woman, that much he was certain of. Devaney had named her and it was not who he had expected. Blair doubted that Devaney would remember in the morning what she had said. At least, he prayed that she didn't but then sighed, knowing he would have to speak with her.

Devaney rose the next morning, searching for Blair, finding him this time at the computer. She could tell he had been there for a while.

"Blair?"

Her voice cut through his thoughts and he looked up, an arm coming out to draw her down on his knee, both arms wrapping around her, a kiss on her forehead. She looked up at that, a frown on her face.

"Blair? What did you do?"

"I found the one who is behind all this. You said the name last night in your nightmares."

"I did? I don't remember." She turned her head, her eyes falling on the photo on the computer monitor, and she paled. "Her?"

"Her. She has the money to do this. None of the others do. They have been her lackies, shall we say, doing what they's been ordered. I sent the name on to Dallas and Will. They have promised to find her." He sighed, his arms tightening around her. "I also sent it to Barnabas and Breck. They're tightening up security here, to make sure she can't get through."

"I pray she doesn't but how do we know? She could change her looks, play the victim."

"Barnabas has thought of that. He has asked that we stay inside for the next few days. That will be so hard on you." He studied her face. "And no, we're not putting you out there."

———

"I know, but somehow I think that's what it will take. She'll stay hidden, and we'll have no life until she's found."

"Will mentioned that. If we are out, we have officers with us. Barnabas has brought in more security for here."

"He can't!"

"It's already done. Breck was by here earlier with Branigan. They'll all take as many precautions as they can. We'll end this." He looked over as his phone chimed and he tilted it to read the message. "Well, well. Dallas works fast. He's found her."

"He has? Wonderful!"

Chapter 52

Devaney moved quickly through the book store, looking for a particular book, finding it and then heading for the cashier, ready to walk away. Her steps slowed as she approached, not seeing the woman. She turned and began to run for the back door, sliding to a stop at the appearance of a woman. She backed away, hitting a table behind her, unable to move any further away.

"Well, well. Who do we have here?" The woman's arm was extended, a pistol pointing at Devaney. "You'll not get away this time. All these years, I have been tracking you, finding you, only to have you get away from me. It's not happening this time. This time, you pay."

"I don't understand, Alice. Why?"

"Do I need a reason? You're why Jerry had to leave that foster home. I had him placed there, but they didn't keep him, sent him away after a couple of hours."

"How could that be my fault? I was only, what, ten?"

"They said they didn't have room for him. They should have let you go."

Devaney's horror grew. "You're the one."

"The one, what?"

"The one that caused their accident. That's why I had to leave."

"So what? No one will ever know. It's just you and me here." Alice Green moved forward again, stopping just a few feet away from Devaney.

Devaney edged sideways from the table, watching her closely. If I can get away from her, maybe I can run. The pistol moving to point at her head stopped her.

The two woman stood, neither moving, neither speaking. Afterwards, Devaney could not tell for how long that had been. She sensed movement behind Alice, not moving her eyes from the older woman, not willing to be shot for this woman. Devaney frowned, trying to piece together how Alice fit into it all.

She looked up a bit as she saw a shadow moving towards Alice, catching sight of the police officers, dropping to the floor at a motion from them, scrambling away under the table. Her hands covered her ears as she huddled down, not wanting to move. She heard the screams and curses and vile language spouting from Alice and shuddered, knowing just how close it had been. She didn't move as she heard footsteps around her, shifting away from the hands reaching for her, sobs rising within her, tears flowing down her face.

Will stood and watched, his heart breaking for Devaney, knowing they wouldn't reach her. He turned and walked to the door and then outside, his eyes searching before he walked to the police line.

"Will?" Blair was hardly able to speak.

―――

"She's alive but shut down. We can't reach her. Come with me. It's an unusual set of circumstances but given what she's been through and what you both have been through, I need you to come with me. You'll be the only one to reach through to her."

Blair stood for a moment, his eyes on Will before they moved to the store, seeing Alice being led away in handcuffs, and then the store clerk helped out and to an ambulance. "Suzy?"

"She was knocked out. She wasn't out for long and heard what Alice said. That's good, in a way. We have an eyewitness so Alice is not going to be able to get off."

Blair's steps slowed as he approached the table, seeing the crumpled and huddled form of his wife. An word from Will had the officer stepping back that had stood guard, and Blair dropped to his feet, his hands reaching to gently move Devaney to him, sitting on the floor and cradling her.

Devaney fought the hands that reached for her, desperate to escape, until she heard Blair's voice praying for her. Her arms around his neck, she clung to him, even as sobs still wracked her body. She didn't know that tears flowed down his face as well before he was on his feet, Devaney cradled close to him.

He stood, once again, in the Emergency Department, his eyes on his wife as she was assessed. They had finally given her sedation just to settle her down. Blair hated that she had had to have that. His head turned as he heard footsteps and Branigan appeared.

"Blair?"

"She sleeping. They had to sedate her. That's the only way to settle her down. Is it over?"

"Was she hurt?"

"No, no physically. We'll need to see about counselling for her when she's ready."

"Buckley will do that, or he'll know someone she can talk to. Berneen and Cadee will talk with her."

Blair nodded. "I know they will. Is it really over this time? I can't go through this anymore."

"It's over, Blair." Branigan drew in a deep breath. "Dallas spoke with me on the way in. He's waiting to talk to Devaney but he said tomorrow would work. Will's posted an officer here for the night."

"Thank him for me." Blair paused, his hands rubbing together. "Thank all the guys, Berneen, Cadee, Doc, Anna, the security team, for me. I'll do it when I can, but please let them know we thank them and thank them for the prayers."

"I can do that. Listen, Bradon's going to stay. So is Burnie. Devaney has endeared herself to us all, but particularly to those two."

Blair gave a small grin. "I know she has. Now, to let her heal." He breathed an inaudible thanks to the Lord that he was standing in a hospital and not a funeral home. It could have gone either way, he understood.

———

Chapter 53

A smile on his face, Will watched as Devaney mingled with the group from the Foundation, finally understanding that she was part of the family. He didn't think she had understood that fully before. Barnabas stood beside him, having arranged for the catered meal for them all, and the police officers who had helped. The officers had eaten, stayed for a while, and then left. Other than for Dallas. He and Will needed to finish off their conversation with Devaney and Blair.

Blair approached, his arm around Devaney, who smiled and then reached to hug both Will and Dallas, surprising Dallas as she did so.

"Blair. Devaney. All I can say is that I'm sorry we didn't know about her in time to spare you." Dallas was contrite, thinking he had failed them somehow.

"It's not your fault, Dallas. She hid herself well. I never knew her, but I always felt someone in the background." Devaney leaned back on Blair, his arms around her.

"She was always there. Jerry is her son, but she refused to raise him, to even acknowledge him until he was an adult and useful to her. That's so sad." Dallas paused for a moment. "She did have him placed in that home, Devaney, wanting him to stay there. She had something on that family, but we can't find out what it is. They don't know, and she's not talking. Jerry doesn't now, or won't say. And she did cause the accident they had. That's why you had to be moved. They couldn't look after foster children anymore, not with their injuries."

"That's so sad. They were wonderful people." Devaney reached to brush away a tear. "But what was her motivation towards us?"

"She wanted Bridget to marry Blair and you to marry Jerry, just as you figured. When you two became engaged, she searched for a way to break you up. She didn't know that Blair had accepted work here, not until later. She's the one who chased you across the country, arranging for you to be watched, and yes assaulted. She was behind the stabbing. That water bottle you threw away?"

Devaney nodded. "I wondered about that. Was it really poisoned?"

"It was. God led there. You sensed something wrong and didn't drink from it. She has indicated she put rat poison in it, enough that just a few sips would likely have made you really sick, and without knowing what you had ingested, you wouldn't have received the proper treatment."

Blair shuddered. "I am so thankful God protected Devaney. She could have been gone and I would never have known." He looked at Will and then at Dallas, seeing his friends standing nearby.

"That she could have been." Dallas finally walked away, shaking hands with the gathered men.

Will stood for a moment, his eyes on the younger couple, before he turned to Doc.

"Doc? She's okay now?"

"She's getting there. It will take some time but they're working together on it. They are two parts of a whole." Doc hesitated before he spoke. "You have answered everything?"

"We believe so. Alice was behind everything that happened, including Devaney's wreck that started this all off here, the truck that ran them down, the kidnappings, and then her own attempt at killing Devaney. She's a vicious piece of work."

"And I suspect that you'll find she's done a lot more than this." Barnabas spoke from beside him.

"I'm sure we will. We're reaching out to other forces and finding just that. There will be a lot of work. Those two will have to testify in court, unless she pleads and I don't think she will." Will walked away at long last, a glance back showing the men beginning to leave, Cadee and Berneen hugging Devaney.

Blair was on a hunt. He could not find Devaney anywhere. He was not afraid that she had been kidnapped again. That was in the past by about four months. Blair was thankful that she had not been hurt any worse than she had been, but he still was sad that she had to go through what she did.

He finally tracked her down in one of the gardens. Blair thought to himself he should have known. She liked her outdoors and her flowers. She had taken over the gardens, and Barnabas had willingly let her, knowing they brought healing to her.

Devaney looked up, surprised, then a smile growing on her face as she reached for her husband. She still couldn't believe that they were married. Not after what they had gone through. She knew the trials were still upcoming, only needing to face Alice. She had been told today that all the others had taken plea bargains. Devaney could see God's hand in that.

Blair laughed at her. "Playing in the dirt again, love?"

"Not this time. Just spending time in the garden with my Lord. Gardens have such a wonderful refreshing way with them."

Blair's arms tightened on her as he bent to kiss her. "They do. I think I like the fact that Christ prayed in the garden, and that He prayed for us."

Devaney leaned back to look up at him, seeing his gaze focused in the distance. "I forget that. I need you to remind me every once in a while that is what He did."

They walked for a while, arms around once another, no words necessary before he drew her down on a bench.

"What now, love?"

"What do you mean?" She tilted her head to look up at him.

"What are you planning on doing? I know you don't have to work, but you're not one to keep still."

"I'm not sure. I would like to volunteer somewhere, but I'm not too sure where. Buckley and Barnabas both said they have places and names, but they won't give them to me yet. They say I still need to heal."

"And you do. You've had years of abuse, and it was abuse, to heal from. Just be content where God has placed you at the moment. I know Cadee and Berneen enjoy your company."

"And so does Anna, even though her kitten won't go home." Devaney had a smirk on her face as she said that.

Blair laughed. "No, the little kitty won't go come. You do have to name her, you know."

"I know. I just haven't come up with one yet. I really thought she would be going home, you know."

Blair laughed again as his arms tightened on her, a prayer of thankfulness rising once more within him.

They sat for a while, not seeing the glances from their friends as they passed by, each one thankful that Blair had his love with him and that both had survived.

They finally rose, the sun setting behind them, heading for the building and the potluck meal that Anna had arranged. They would enjoy the meal and companionship of their friends. A question lurked in Devaney's mind, a question as to which one of them would be next and would adventures happen to them all? She prayed for the men's safety as they walked through the unknown future, that God would protect, and that He would bring each one a lady of his own to love   and   cherish.

Dear Readers

Thank you for picking up the story of Blair and his love, Devaney. This one took a long time to write. Neither Blair nor Devaney were willing to share their story with me until the last ten days or so. And even then, I had computer glitches that wiped out a good quantity of what I had written midway through the book.

We are told to seek the Lord and He would be found. Devaney had to relearn that. Her life through the years had driven her faith deep within her, needing Blair to help her find it again.

If that is where you are, feeling like you are wandering in the desert, know that God is with you, that He will be found when you seek Him. My father often spoke of wandering in the desert at times, needing to be refreshed in our walk with God.

God bless each one of you.

Ronna

www.ingramcontent.com/pod-product-compliance
Lightning Source LLC
Chambersburg PA
CBHW061247210726
48293CB00003B/884